Half of Hartwell Hotel

Nikki Perry & Kirsty Roby

1st edition, 2025

Edited by Eva Chan

ISBN 978-1-0670364-2-3 (paperback)

ISBN 978-1-0670364-3-0 (Epub)

Cover design and layout by Yummy Book Covers

Typeset in PT Serif, 10pt

For
Jackie and for Stu

Thank you for showing us your island.

*"Love is the longing for the half
of ourselves we have lost."*
— Milan Kundera, *The Unbearable Lightness of Being*

Disclaimer

Sadly, Agnes Island does not exist, but Stewart Island/ Rakiura, New Zealand's third island, does. If you haven't been, we highly recommend it; for the wildlife, adventure, history and especially the people.

www.stewartisland.co.nz

Māori–English translation

karakia — a Māori prayer to invoke guidance or protection

kia ora — hello, hi

kōwhai — yellow (colour); also a native New Zealand tree with yellow flowers

kuia — an elderly woman, grandmother, female elder

mahi — work, job; or to work, to do a job

mihi whakatau — a formal speech of welcome

mōrena — good morning

rangatira — a Māori chief

tamariki — children

Half of Hartwell Hotel

The Southland Times

World-renowned artist Lawrence Lloyd has died after a short battle with cancer.

Lloyd became a household name in the 1980s after his first exhibition, 'Life on Aggie', sold out in twenty-five minutes and established him as one of New Zealand's most talented expressionist artists. In 1997 his work drew world acclaim when his famous piece 'Scarlet Lady', described by critics as 'a masterpiece of tender love', sold for a then record-breaking nine hundred thousand dollars.

Lloyd lived most of his life on Agnes Island, a remote and sparsely populated island in the far south of New Zealand where he owned a small boutique hotel.

He sold a mere four paintings a year, although rumours persisted that he had a vast collection of works.

His agent, Malcolm Price, said, "Despite his grumpy demeanour, Lloyd was a hugely talented artist, a great friend, and would be sorely missed."

His service will be held at the Holy Trinity Church on Saturday, 22nd of March at 3 pm.

Chapter 1

In her peripheral vision Liv noticed a fan streaking naked across the field, his arse starkly white against the rest of his tan. Speedos, not shorts, she thought, wildly inappropriate to the situation at hand.

At her feet, Connor Reed knelt on the damp turf and the whole stadium had gone eerily silent. His rugby shorts stretched over his thighs, massive with muscle as he pulled out a pale blue box. Liv could feel the sports network cameras zooming in on her face and her heart felt like it was beating in her throat.

A group of cheerleaders came onto the field behind them, dancing to the Bruno Mars song that had started to play. The rest of the team joined in, then the ref, the coach, even the ball boys. A well-choreographed flash mob.

Overhead, a plane engine thrummed, trailing a huge banner.

"Well?" Connor asked, his famously cheeky grin huge on his movie star handsome face. "Will you marry me, Olivia

Peterson?" He opened the box, the camera guy focusing in on the sparkling diamond nestled inside, projected up on the big screen. It was so huge he really needn't have bothered; Liv was fairly certain even the pilot could see it.

The crowd went wild, screaming and cheering. A chant started up. "Say yes, say yes, say yes." There was a record number of bums on seats today — it was a big game and the All Blacks needed this win. Connor waited expectantly, confidence oozing from him. Liv's stomach churned like a vat of sewage, sweat pooling in her pits. Looking around at all the eyes expectantly waiting on her answer, she turned back to her boyfriend of almost two years and swallowed.

"Connor, no," she said quietly, except there was a news reporter there, holding a fluffy mic out towards her, making the 'no' horribly loud, echoing slightly in the stadium. A collective gasp went up and then Liv bolted. She ran for her life, past the reporters and cameras and the VIP box of WAGS and minor celebrities, past the incredulous faces of Connor's parents, with the crowd's thunderous booing and disgust following behind her.

Of course, the paparazzi followed her. After ten minutes, dashing down side streets and through a children's playground, she'd only managed to lose about half of them. Despite being thankful for all those tedious hours on the treadmill at the gym, she deeply regretted her choice of footwear.

When did she become the type of girl who wore heels to the rugby anyway? She'd left her phone and bag behind in Connor's BMW, so there was no way to call an Uber, or someone to get her, even if she did have someone who would.

Ahead, there was a church. Never had Liv been so pleased to see one. Surely they couldn't follow her in there?

In the foyer she stopped to catch her breath. It was cooler inside, all white wood, stained glass and the flickering of candles. It smelled faintly of incense. Soft music played and Liv eyed up the holy water, mouth parched. Through an ornate stained-glass window by the door, she could see two paparazzi lurking near the church gate.

Scuttling as quietly as possible up the aisle, she took a seat in one of the pews near the back. There were only two other people in the room, a man in the front row wearing a dark jacket, his head bent, and the priest who was standing to the side at a podium.

Then she noticed the coffin.

Of course she had somehow managed to gatecrash a funeral, because it wasn't enough that she had turned down New Zealand's most beloved All Black and the whole country probably hated her right now.

Connor knew she didn't want to get married. She had been trying to break up with him for weeks, and she was sure he'd done it intentionally, proposing so publicly, trying to force her to agree. Except she hadn't.

Now here she was, stuck in a church listening to the eulogy for some guy called Lawrence that she'd never met, and since there was only one other person here, she could hardly leave unnoticed, could she?

While the priest talked, she tried to come up with a plan. She needed to get past the reporters first, somehow get back to the apartment and get her stuff. Only where was she going to go?

She should never have given up her flat. Never have agreed to move in with Connor. She could maybe sleep the night at Lea's, except since she'd had Archie she had no spare room, and Liv couldn't camp on her sofa for more than a night or two. She wasn't close enough to any of her other friends to ask and when she thought about it, most of them were likely to side with Connor anyway. Her dad would make up an excuse because of his wife Laura and the boys and in any case he lived too far away from her work.

Shit, work. Would she even have a job after this? Even if Connor still wanted her as his PR agent, she doubted his father, who owned the company, would want to keep her on.

So the country now hated her, she probably had no job and she had nowhere to live. Great. The last place she wanted to go was to her mum's, but she probably didn't have a choice, at least for now. The thought made her want to cry.

Speaking of which, was the guy in front crying? She felt

terrible sitting there worrying about her own issues while he grieved. There was a photo of who she assumed was the deceased in a frame atop the coffin. A small, wiry old guy with a fierce scowl. Liv watched the dark-haired guy in front, wondering if this was his grandfather.

How depressing, to have only one person turn up to your funeral. She wondered how many would bother to come to hers? Would anyone? As she stood to sing a hymn, she sniffed loudly to stop herself from crying. The guy turned to look at her, then looked away.

The service was short and once it finished, Liv headed towards the exit, only to be stopped by a reed-thin woman with a scraped-back bun.

"If you wouldn't mind signing the register?" She indicated towards a hall table where a hardback book sat, open to the first page. It was too complicated to explain why she was really there, so Liv picked up the pen and signed her name, mobile number and email address on the first line, then added 'My condolences' as an afterthought.

Glancing through the window, Liv saw no sign of the reporters. It looked like they had given up and left. That was a relief.

"How did you know Laurie?"

Liv turned to find the dark-haired guy looking at her as he added his name below hers.

"Umm, gosh, let me think," Liv said. "I think it was the dog park?" Why she said that, she wasn't sure. She didn't even have a dog. Never had. Her mother had never let her have a pet. Too dirty. Liv had just panicked.

"That's odd, Laurie was always more of a cat person back in the day." The man looked pensive. "What sort of dog did he have?"

"On second thought, no, not the park," Liv said. "Maybe the café?"

"Right, is there one on the island now?"

"The island?"

"Aggie." He raised an eyebrow. "Agnes Island?"

"Aggie, yes, right. Could be. Although, actually ..." Liv laughed awkwardly. "To be honest, I don't really know Laurie all *that* well."

"I see." He frowned slightly, furrows forming between his eyes. He was a nice-looking guy, clean-shaven with kind eyes and a light smattering of freckles that made it hard to guess his age. "Okay, so were you more a fan of his work?"

Liv chewed on one of her newly manicured nails. Nails that Connor had insisted she had done yesterday, which now made sense. She had no idea what this guy was referring to and she could feel her cheeks burning.

"Not as such ..." she hedged.

"Sorry, my apologies, I'm Ambrose. Ambrose McCafferty. I used to spend my summers on Aggie." He reached out a large hand and she took it. His palm was warm and she noticed a bracelet on his wrist, cheap plastic beads spelling out something on nylon thread. It seemed at odds with the rest of him, his tidy haircut, well-fitted suit and cufflinks. Liv wondered if he had a child who had made it for him.

"Liv," she told him. "Olivia Peterson."

He smiled slightly and looked around the church, then back to her. "Not a great turnout, is it?" he said. "I know he was a bit of a loner, but I had thought a few more people might come."

"Right, yes. It is a bit surprising, since he was such a great guy. A real laugh." Ambrose gave her a strange look. "I can't imagine there would be many people who would agree with you," he said. "When did you last see him?"

"Gosh, it has to be, what?" Liv tried to look thoughtful, as if she was tallying up days or months on a mental calendar, but she was a terrible liar. She felt like a possum in the headlights. She couldn't do it. "Look, I actually came in here to get away from the reporters," she blurted. "I turned down a proposal and this seemed like a good place to hide."

"Right." The frown deepened.

Liv felt like she had as a child, sent to the principal's office for misbehaving. "Sorry," she muttered.

"Well, I have to get back," Ambrose said, looking at his watch. "It was ..." he trailed off. "Well, good luck," and it might be her imagination, but did his voice seem colder? He gave her a quick nod and then headed towards the door.

"I don't suppose you could call me a cab?" Liv called after him and he stopped, pausing for a beat before he turned.

"I don't bring my phone to funerals." His voice was most

definitely colder than before. "Or go to them when I don't know the deceased, actually."

Outside, as she set off for the long walk home, a blister forming at her heel, it started to rain.

Perfect funeral weather, Liv noted.

Chapter 2

The paparazzi had finally stopped camping outside Liv's mother's house. This felt like the only good news for the day after another fruitless attempt to get a job in an industry that Renfield Reed had blacklisted her from.

The antiseptic smell hit her as she opened the front door, cloyingly familiar. Liv removed her shoes and socks, before sliding on a pair of house slippers. She took off her pants and top and wrapped herself into a cotton robe from the hall cupboard. After sanitising her hands from the pump bottle on the side table, she gathered her clothes and padded down the plastic floor runner to the laundry.

"Did you spray your shoes?" her mother called from the lounge and Liv only barely held back her irritation. She knew her mother wasn't well. That it wasn't her fault, this ridiculous obsession with germs, but after six long weeks of living in the equivalent of a hospital bubble, the strain of it all was getting to be overwhelming.

"No, but I'll do it now," Liv called back as she put her clothes into the machine.

It was hard to remember a time when her mother wasn't like this, but there was a period when Liv was young where she didn't know that it wasn't normal to be forbidden to use public toilets, or touch the shopping trolley until it had been gone over with a disinfectant wipe, or that other people didn't wipe down the groceries before they put them away.

Once upon a time her mother had run the house as a bed and breakfast, welcoming guests in as a way to support them after her dad left, but gradually the idea of strangers coming into the house was too much for her mother to cope with. It had become so bad that she barely left the house anymore, afraid of the outside world and its germs.

"How did the interview go?" Deirdre had beaten her to the shoes, holding out Liv's heels in gloved hands and spraying the soles with disinfectant. After six weeks, Liv imagined Deirdre was probably almost as desperate to get rid of her daughter as Liv was to leave.

"Not great." Liv headed into the kitchen. "I think maybe it's time to look at some other options." She opened the fridge and pulled out her bottle of Riesling. "Want one?"

Deirdre nodded, going over to the cabinet and getting the glasses. "What other options?" she asked, inspecting the rim of one glass and then reaching for a clean dishcloth to ensure its spotlessness.

"Hospitality maybe?" Liv hated the thought of going back to waitressing — she'd done the hard yards as a student — but she would if she had to. "I might be able to get some bar work." She poured the wine and tried not to gulp hers down too quickly as she headed towards the lounge with her handbag, fishing in it for her phone. "I saw an ad yesterday for a new place called The Sawdust Saloon."

"Oh Livvy, that sounds very unhygienic." Deirdre sounded as if Liv had suggested she might work at the local sewage treatment sewage treatment plant. "And please, wipe down your phone. There are over 17,000 bacteria on the average mobile device." She handed Liv a disinfectant wipe from a stack beside her chair.

Liv had never much liked Connor's penthouse apartment, which had been decorated by a designer and felt showy and impersonal, but now, she almost missed it. Almost.

According to the gossip mags, Connor was 'devastated'. But he hadn't tried to contact her since the proposal. She'd tried calling him to apologise but he'd blocked her number. There didn't seem much point to keep trying. He was clearly done with her.

There was a text message on her phone from Sean Anthony, one of her clients. He wanted to meet her to discuss something. Probably to tell her he couldn't keep her on as his publicist. She didn't blame him, but she would be sad to lose him. He'd been a good friend as well as a client and she'd known him for a long time now, spending time with him and his wife Karen and even holidaying with them and their kids.

She was about to text him back when her phone rang. It wasn't a number she recognised and she'd had a few nasty calls from die-hard rugby fans, but it could also be about the job, so she answered it tentatively.

"Hello, Liv speaking ..."

"Is this Olivia Peterson?"

"It is," Liv confirmed, reaching over to put her glass down on the side table beside the couch as she sat, the protective plastic cover sticking to her thighs.

"This is Jeanie from Crompton, Simpson and Baker, attorneys at law. Did you happen to attend the funeral of Mr Lawrence Lloyd on Saturday the 22nd of March?"

Liv thought back to that day, the awful moment of Connor's proposal, the long walk back to her mother's house from the church, and the disapproving face of Ambrose McCafferty that had stuck with her for some reason she couldn't quite fathom.

"I did, yes, but I was trying to avoid the reporters and I didn't realise—" but Jeanie cut her off.

"Mr Crompton would like to speak to you about Mr Lloyd's estate and his final wishes," she said. "Are you available sometime this week to schedule a meeting?"

"I didn't actually know Mr Lloyd," Liv said. "I was just—"

"Nevertheless, if you could meet with Mr Crompton, say Thursday at eleven? Would that suit?"

"Well, okay, but I'm not sure that—"

"Perfect, Mr Crompton will see you then. I'll email you confirmation and the address."

The phone call disconnected before Liv could reply.

Sean gave her another long hug and Liv tried not to cry against his Hugo Boss shirt.

"I really am sorry," he said again. "I'm serious about changing over to you as my PR once my contract with these pricks is up. And if there's ever anything I can do to help ..."

There was a flash and a series of clicks and they pulled away from each other. Across the road from her mother's driveway, a photographer was taking snaps.

"You fucking tosser," Sean called out, stepping away from Liv to head across the road.

"Don't, Sean, it's not worth it." Liv grabbed his hand to stop him. "They'll only take more. But you should probably go."

"I suppose you're right." He gave her hand a squeeze before he started across the road. "Bloody wanker," he muttered at the photographer as he got into his Bentley. "Talk soon, Livvy."

As he drove off, Liv looked over at the camera guy who was now getting into his own little car, the door hinge squeaking as he closed it. She looked down at her running gear, wishing they wouldn't keep catching her at her worst. Still, at least she was dressed. There had been a time at Connor's when they'd managed to get her in a towel out on his terrace, her hair in a messy pile on top of her head, looking like she'd come straight from a romp in the sheets, when in reality she'd been rescuing a hedgehog that had fallen in the lap pool.

She'd stopped looking at social media anyway, sick of all the headlines blaming her for the All Blacks' losses and Connor's supposed heartbreak. They had painted her as a gold-digging villain, despite the fact that if she was after his money, surely she would have said yes to his proposal?

Half the country hated her. She'd had abuse and even death threats through her social media until she finally turned them off. She'd lost her job, most of her so-called friends had ditched her, and Connor had trashed most of her stuff from the flat before she'd had a chance to get in and pack. Not that she had much use for designer cocktail dresses anymore, but she could have sold most of them since she was now dangerously low in savings.

The world saw her as the girl who had broken Connor Reed's heart. He'd had an appallingly bad season ever since that day. He'd even done a magazine spread, claiming Liv had ruined him. It was all bull. Their relationship had been rocky for a long time.

She'd never been desperate to date him, especially since

she worked for his father, but Connor, she had discovered, loved a challenge. He could be charming and charismatic. He'd worn her down and suddenly they'd gone from 'just dinner' to dating in the public eye and moving in together. Liv had told him repeatedly that she felt it was all a bit fast and that she wasn't ready for any serious commitment, but Connor never took no for an answer. He was used to getting his own way, to having 'yes men' around him and people fawning over him.

Then there was the recreational drug use. His, not hers. And the niggling feeling she had that he wasn't exactly being faithful. Only the week before his proposal they had discussed taking a break. He had to have known she didn't want to get engaged, which is exactly why he'd put her on the spot like that, in front of hundreds of thousands of people.

Now, she was screwed, living at home with her hypochondriac mother, with no job, no money and a reputation for being a heartless bitch. Still, at least she was free, she thought, as she took off for her run. But free to do what?

Chapter 3

There was a kākā on the front veranda when Ambose opened the door and stepped out into the cool of the early morning, coffee cup in hand. The parrot shuffled expectantly along the railing, bobbing slightly, its claws scraping loudly against the flaking red wood.

"Good morning, Lester." Ambrose reached into his pants pocket and then laid a flat palm out in offering. The bird came forward, stretching out a large claw, and daintily extracted a sunflower seed from the small pile with its beak.

It was bitterly cold. The sea was foaming and churning, the wind off it sharp on his skin. Out on the horizon the small ferry rolled and pitched. Ambrose was surprised to see it; on days like this it was usually cancelled, the sea too rough to cross. Winters on Aggie Island were not for the faint of heart.

Ambrose had never felt happier.

He had been at work when he got the phone call. Sitting at his desk dealing with a truant child, a backlog of reports to the Ministry of Education to sign, scrambling for relievers for the next day, and wishing he was anywhere but there.

He'd loved his job when he first got his teaching degree. Loved making a difference to kids, like some of his teachers had done for him. He'd found it challenging, rewarding and stimulating in equal measure. But as he rose up the ranks he began to lose sight of why he'd become a teacher in the first place.

His mother had been thrilled when he became deputy principal. Especially because it was Saint George, a prestigious, private, all-boys school with world acclaim. She had told him at every opportunity that he would be principal before he hit forty. The idea made his heart sink.

He loved teaching — hands on, not all the admin and politics of running a school. Those days where he had to fill in for a sick teacher were the best. So when he got that phone call from the lawyers, the decision was easy.

"You've inherited half of Mr Lloyd's estate, including the hotel," the solicitor had told him, sitting behind his mahogany desk, peering over his spectacles. "The will stipulates that anyone who turned up to his funeral service would get an equal share of the Hartwell Hotel, situated on Agnes Island. It's you and one other beneficiary, so a fifty-fifty share."

That one other had to be that woman who'd only come in to escape from the media. Olivia Peterson. She didn't even know Laurie. Sure, Ambrose wasn't a relative either, and he hadn't been to Agnes Island since he'd lost touch with Mike when they went to separate colleges, but Ambrose remembered his time on the island with such fondness. Those days were the highlight of his youth really, after growing up in a home where he was raised more by his nannies than his parents.

His friendship with Mike had been a lifesaver. Spending summer holidays at Mike's grandfather's house had been magical and Ambrose couldn't believe he was back here. He could still remember the fun they had had as kids at this hotel, running wild and free.

He'd lost touch with Mike when he went to boarding school, and had only heard about his accident after he had run into another classmate, long after the funeral. But he'd thought about him and Laurie numerous times over the years.

The decision to throw in his job and come back to Aggie had been instinctive. He'd handed in his notice, packed up his apartment and put it on the market, taken the essentials and left. He felt as if he were leaving nothing of importance behind. And now here he was, back where he felt the most at home, half owner of a hotel. A very run-down hotel, but Ambrose could remember how it had been. With a little bit of work, he was sure it could be transformed back to the grand old lady it had been when he was a child.

The ferry had pulled up to the dock and Ambrose could see in the distance Weeble stepping off in his gumboots and Swanndri, long speckled beard almost down to his belly. He tied the boat up to the pilings with a practised ease and then unlatched the side door. A few people disembarked. Ambrose recognised the lumbering gait of Glenn as he ambled over to help Weeble with the luggage, then the distinctive red head of the local cop Tom and his big shaggy dog, Lad. One of the Banks kids — Ambrose couldn't tell which one — sloped off, a bag slung over their shoulder, heading towards the town.

After a few minutes, a woman stepped gingerly off, clinging to the side of the dock for a minute and then lurching towards the little office before she stopped, hunching over a rubbish bin and heaving. She was wearing a jacket with a fur-trimmed hood and boots with a sizeable heel. Ambrose watched as she retrieved her bags from the steel bin that had been offloaded. She hefted out two large suitcases that she pulled along the rickety dock with some difficulty, her handbag on one shoulder.

It was her. That woman from the funeral. He was surprised to see her. Ambrose had been on the island for three weeks already and had decided she probably wasn't interested in anything but a payout for her half of the hotel. Yet here she was, ridiculously dressed, and with far too much baggage for his liking.

He should go down to the dock and offer to help. Or send Howie in the car, although the way Howie drove she would likely beat him. But instead, Ambrose watched her struggle along the main street, his euphoric mood dissolving into a rising resentment.

He wanted this hotel. Wanted this life on the island that felt like a home to him. He didn't need the complication of this high-maintenance woman. He'd googled her. She was all over the news, stories of her lavish lifestyle, her refusal of that proposal, her rumoured affair with some actor, incriminating photos of them together surfacing mere weeks after she'd turned down Connor Reed.

There was a nudge against his leg and he looked down to see Mr Tiddles, Laurie's cat. He was part of the inheritance deal. No selling the hotel until the seemingly much-loved feline died. Funny, Laurie hadn't been much of a people person but he loved cats. Ambrose was slightly allergic, but the old tabby seemed to prefer to be mostly outside, and so far, it was working out fine.

He looked back at Olivia. She had stopped to talk to Mrs Allen who was pointing up the hill to the hotel. She looked up the steep, potholed road and her shoulders visibly slumped. She was not the type of woman Ambrose could see lasting on a small island with a population of only two hundred and sixty-five people. There were no fancy bars or designer clothing stores, no nightclubs or trendy cafés. She would probably take one look at the run-down hotel, looking even bleaker in the drizzle that had now started, and take the next ferry home, he thought. He hoped.

Chapter 4

Liv felt queasy the whole ferry trip. It started almost as soon as they hit the first big swell. She stood outside on the deck, knowing fresh air was the best preventative for seasickness, but less than an hour in to the almost two-hour trip, she was leaning over the railing, next to the large steel bin that held the luggage, heaving up her toast and marmalade and English Breakfast tea. In the distance, Agnes Island was nothing but a small, green blob. The sky was an ominous grey, the sort that felt like a permanent feature, that perhaps the sun might never make an appearance this far south.

Her sole companion on deck, a solid, freckled man with reddish hair poking out of his beanie, with a large shaggy dog at his side, handed her a crumpled tissue from the pocket of his jacket. She thanked him, then turned to puke up the rest of her breakfast into the churning sea.

Once the steel bin had been offloaded, she retrieved her luggage with the help of a smiling man in a plaid Swanndri, then made her way down the jetty. The small area adjacent was, according to a carved sign on the beachfront, the township of Hartwell. 'Township', however, seemed a bit of a stretch. It was really no more than a road with a couple of offshoots, running through a small cluster of container buildings and wooden shops with old-fashioned frontages, offset by a tiny school, a mechanic's with a petrol bowser, and a community hall. Down one of the offshoot roads, Liv could see what looked like a small medical centre, a police office and a fire station. That was it. It was eerily quiet and a little like she had travelled back in time.

After Liv stopped in at the store for a bottle of ginger beer to settle her stomach, Bridie Allen, the weather-worn proprietor, pointed her in the direction of the hotel. Apparently, there was only one taxi driver, and he was nowhere to be seen. The building was perched on a hill overlooking the harbour up a steep gravel road. There was no footpath. Liv pulled her hood up against the light rain and dragged her suitcases behind her, a duffel bag balanced on each one, and set off determinedly up the road. She had to stop every so often to hoist her handbag further up her shoulder and adjust her grip on the handles. From a distance, the hotel wasn't at all what she had been expecting, smaller and not as grand, and it looked like it wasn't in great shape.

When she'd found out that she'd inherited half of a hotel after attending the funeral of a man she'd never met, Liv had thought there must have been some kind of mistake. Mr Lloyd's lawyers had insisted, despite her protests that she'd only ended up in the church accidentally, that those were the terms of the will and she was now the part owner of one Hartwell Hotel on Agnes Island, a remote place she'd never visited.

The press hadn't let up hounding her since photos of her hugging Sean outside her house had been published. They'd even dug up an old photograph from the previous year of Sean with his arm around Liv in a dimly lit restaurant, conveniently cutting off his wife who had been on his other side. It didn't matter that he'd since been photographed holidaying in Fiji with his wife Karen, sharing a double hammock and with happy smiles. Naysayers had said the holiday photos were all for PR, to save his reputation, despite the fact they'd been happily married for years without a single whisper of any previous cheating rumours. Liv was now branded a homewrecker and a cheating hussy as well as a gold-digger. So here she was, about as far away as she could get without leaving the country, the perfect place to hole up away from the prying eyes of the paps.

She was drenched in sweat when she rounded the final corner. The hood of her coat had blown back and her hair was plastered to her face. Icy drops of rain trickled unpleasantly down the back of her coat. Liv stopped and took a good look at the hotel she now owned half of. Close up, it was even more run down. There was a wide veranda across the front overlooking the ocean, which would be the perfect place to sit with a beer in the summer, if summer was even a thing here. It seemed impossible to visualise right now. At this time of year, the weathered wooden tables were empty. Some of the chairs leant tipsily and looked like they could be a hazard. The building had originally been painted red but it was peeling badly, like skin that had seen too much sun. The hotel had two storeys with a narrower balcony running the length of the first floor. Large windows at the bottom, probably the bar area, were filmy with salt from the sea. There were steps leading up to the front door but no ramp. Liv sighed and pulled her bags up the uneven front path. The door opened.

"Mōrena, you look like you need a hand, love." A man with a wild scrub of steel-grey hair and a beard to match came down the steps towards her. His face, or what you could see of it through the excess facial hair, was deeply wrinkled and he was wearing mismatched work socks with no shoes.

"Gordo." He held out a hand for her to shake, then noticed her staring at his feet. "Left my gumboots somewhere. No clue where they've got to."

Liv shook his hand, which was a bit grubby. She surreptitiously wiped hers on her jeans, while Gordo grabbed hold of the handle of one of her bags and lugged it up the short flight of steps.

"Blimey, what have you got in here? Rocks?"

"Something like that." Liv hefted the other suitcase up after him.

Gordo held the door open for her and then once they'd got all her luggage inside, closed it behind them. "Bit nippy out there today," he said.

It wasn't much warmer inside. Liv felt the sweat that had been pooling in her armpits cooling rapidly.

"No idea where Ambrose has buggered off to." Gordo scratched his woolly beard. "He was here before, watching the ferry come in. I'll see if I can find him for you."

He ambled off and Liv shrugged off her wet jacket. She was standing in a gloomy reception area, dimly lit by a dusty chandelier with one remaining bulb, the walls painted a deep forest green. Probably about fifty years ago. To one side was a door to the bar and on the right was another, to the restaurant, which was currently closed. A staircase swept up to the second floor. It would have been fairly impressive in its day, but the handrail was scratched and worn and many of the balusters were broken. It was the same with the reception desk, a beautiful piece of kauri that hadn't seen any care for some time. There was no elevator.

She opened a further door to peer inside what turned out to be the office and someone cleared their throat behind her. When she spun around she saw Ambrose McCafferty, the man from the funeral, with Gordo behind him.

In her memory from that day Ambrose loomed in his dark suit, a tall figure of a man with a perpetual frown and look of disapproval. Even without the suit, in jeans and a thick argyle jumper, there was still the frown and disapproving expression. Liv's memory had skipped the part where he also had broad shoulders, tapering to narrow hips and long legs and, if he hadn't been frowning, a rather handsome face.

"Olivia, isn't it?" he said. Unlike Gordo, he didn't offer a hand to shake. "I didn't expect you to show up."

"And not claim my half of this lovely heritage building?" She felt her face flush at the thought she'd been caught snooping. The office door was still open behind her. "And please, call me Liv."

Ambrose swept his eyes over her pile of luggage. Liv wished for a moment that her suitcases were a sensible black rather than pink. Ambrose was definitely the type of person who would have black suitcases. Even if it meant he had to check every name tag on the carousel to locate his bags, among all the other identical black ones. The way he was eyeing up her belongings, you'd have thought she'd brought enough luggage for a small tour group. This was almost everything she owned, since her mother hadn't wanted her to leave anything behind, causing any unnecessary mess or clutter.

Ambrose tapped his fingers impatiently against the reception counter. "A bit of notice would have been nice. I suppose we can put you in number two, though I'm sure you'll be very disappointed. Gordo can show you to your room."

Gordo backed towards the door of the bar. "Sorry, mate, I'd better get back to work."

Liv got a glimpse of the almost empty bar as he disappeared through the door.

"He's the bar manager?" she asked.

Ambrose grunted. "I guess you could call him that, at a stretch." He fished a key with a wooden tag from a hook on the wall behind the reception counter and handed it to her. It was the old-fashioned type, one of those iron skeleton keys. It looked generic, like you'd be able to use it in any of the doors. Clearly no key cards here.

"Upstairs, through the door, take the right-hand passage. It's at the end."

Liv thought he was going to leave her to it, but he glanced up the stairs, then back at her bags and seemed to have second thoughts, sighed and gripped the handle of the nearest case, which happened to be the lightest one.

The stairs creaked and groaned like they were protesting as they made their way up. There were two flights, separated by a landing. The carpet runner was thin and loose, which made it hard work when it came to lifting the heavy bags. At the top, Liv paused. She had the impression of dark wood everywhere. Dark wood doors. Dark wood floors. Wooden panelling on the bottom half of the walls, the top painted a sickly yellow. Or had it once been cream? Ambrose was striding down a hallway to the right, easily pulling her bag behind him, so she hurried after him as best she could. They went around a corner and down another hallway before Ambrose stopped outside room number two.

"Bathroom's the next door along. It's shared," he said. "No doubt you're used to having your own en suite. The door doesn't lock so you'll find a tag on the inside handle. Hang that outside when you're using it."

"What are the restaurant hours?" Liv asked. She was still feeling a bit queasy from the ferry ride, but after a hot shower and a rest, she'd need something to eat.

"The winter hours are Thursday through till Sunday. It's unfortunate that today is Wednesday." Ambrose had a satisfied expression on his face, as though seeing Liv go hungry was the highlight of his day. What was this man's problem? They'd barely exchanged two sentences at the funeral and, okay, he'd caught Liv out in a tiny little white lie, but she'd been flustered. If he'd been proposed to in public and then hunted down like a rabbit by the paparazzi, Ambrose might not have put his best foot forward either.

"Well, I imagine I can get something to eat at the shop." She didn't fancy another walk down the hill in the rain, and it came out a little snappy.

"You can probably get something at the bar, if you're not averse to a bowl of chips or a toasted sandwich. Let Gordo know, any time after five-thirty." Then he turned on his heel and strode back down the hallway, disappearing around the corner.

Liv let herself into her room, propped one bag against the door to keep it open, which turned out to be unnecessary, and then dragged the rest of her stuff inside. The room was on the small side, with a double bed pushed against one wall, a single bedside cabinet with a rickety lamp precariously balanced on top and a wardrobe which had a shabby salmon-coloured curtain in place of a door. The heavily patterned wallpaper was designed for a room of a much grander scale and there was a stale, musty smell as if it had been unused for some time. Liv crossed to the window, feeling disoriented but hoping for a view of the ocean at least. Her room was located in a wing of the hotel towards the back and looked down onto a kind of unkempt courtyard. On the wing opposite she could see a fire escape leading up to one of the sash windows. It didn't look like it would hold the weight of a toddler and she hoped like hell there wouldn't be a fire any time soon. The hotel clearly hadn't had any work done to it for a long time. Sighing, Liv flipped open her suitcase and found her toiletries. Closing the door behind her, she padded down the hallway to the bathroom.

There had been no towels in the room but she was thankful to find a stack on a chair in the corner of the bathroom. It was actually a pretty decent size with a lot of wasted space. Liv crossed to the shower stall, pulled back the translucent curtain and peered in. It was old but clean, at least. She turned on the mixer. Lovely hot steam soon filled the room. As Ambrose had said, the door didn't lock but she found the little tag stating that the room was occupied on the back of the door and hung it on the front handle. It was a bit odd, not being able to lock the door, but she had to trust in the process. She hadn't seen any guests around in any case. Liv dropped her damp clothes onto the floor and stepped into the warm water with a happy sigh.

Staying under the hot water as long as she could, she washed off the grime of the journey, reluctant to get out into the cold air, but eventually hunger won out. She wrapped herself in her towel and scuttled quickly back to her room. The easiest clothes to locate were a pair of black trousers and a pink mohair jumper at the top of her case; a little dressy for a Wednesday night perhaps, but she'd unpack and rearrange everything later.

She put her boots back on, hoping to get something to eat at the bar. Ambrose was doing something behind the reception desk and looked up as she came downstairs. If he'd looked disgruntled before, his face now was like thunder.

"Are you aware," he said through gritted teeth, "that you are on an island?"

"Given that I spent two hours on a ferry puking my guts out, I—"

"And that we don't have an unlimited supply of hot water?" He stood with his arms crossed, his eyebrows almost knit together. "The entire island is powered by diesel generators. The diesel is shipped from the mainland. It's a costly exercise. If you're used to hour-long showers every night, you can forget about that right now. There's no space for that kind of extravagance on Aggie."

"Okay, sorry, but how was I supposed to know that?" Liv said, trying to keep her voice even. She felt furious and humiliated. Had he been standing outside the door timing her? He was also wildly exaggerating the time she'd taken. "Maybe there should be a notice in the bathroom to let the guests know that there will be an extra charge for every extra minute they spend in the shower."

"That's not a guest bathroom," Ambrose said, turning back to whatever he'd been doing.

As she slunk past him into the bar, Liv decided she'd need to check the guest bathrooms to see whether there was indeed a sign moderating guest use of hot water. It wouldn't surprise her. Maybe that, along with the general state of the place, explained why there didn't seem to be many people staying at the hotel.

Chapter 5

Liv woke to the sound of pitiful meowing and scratching at her door. She checked her phone and was surprised to see it was almost eight. Streaks of grey light peeked through the gap in her curtains. It was going to be another miserable day. She opened the door and peered blearily down at a dishevelled, tabby cat.

"Mr Tiddles, I presume." She bent to give him a pat. Mr Tiddles rewarded her with a hiss and deep growl.

Sighing, Liv turned on her light, a single bulb hanging low and dim from the water-stained ceiling, then located her dressing gown and slippers. The cat waited patiently outside the open doorway, then padded after her as she made her way down the hallway.

Nobody had bothered to give her a tour of the hotel so once she was downstairs she tried the door to the bar, which was locked. The restaurant was open though. There were about half a dozen tables, the old Formica kind that were popular mid-century, with brightly painted tins holding cutlery and serviettes. Liv could hear voices beyond this so she made her way behind the deserted restaurant and into the kitchen.

"… and then he said; 'Well, I'd be more than happy for a repeat of last night', and I had half an hour before the ferry, so …"

"Simon! I don't need to hear that …"

The couple in the kitchen stopped talking as Liv appeared in the doorway.

"Sorry," the woman said, smoothing a hand across dark hair, pulled back tightly from her forehead. "Breakfast won't be ready for another hour." She smiled kindly at Liv. "Guests aren't really allowed in the kitchen."

"Oh, right. I'm not actually a guest. I'm Liv. Liv Peterson."

The woman stared politely at Liv, but looked puzzled.

"I'm the second owner of the hotel." She felt like a fraud as she said it. The cat brushed up against her legs, reminding her of his existence. "I think the cat's hungry. Can you show me where I can find his food?"

Mr Tiddles and his well-being was a condition of the will. This Lawrence Lloyd character had obviously been a bit odd. His stipulation was that the hotel could not be sold as long as Mr Tiddles was alive. Mr Tiddles looked remarkably healthy and rather plump, despite his grumpy demeanour. This could put a spanner in Liv's plans.

The woman wiped her hands on her apron and stepped forward. "I'm afraid Ambrose hadn't told us anything about you." She held out a hand. "I'm Celia. I run the kitchen and this is my brother, Simon."

"I *don't* run the kitchen," Simon said, "but I guess you could say I'm the bottle washer, cleaner and general dogs-body." He came forward and Liv was about to hold her hand out for him to shake too, but he surprised her by coming in for a hug. "Welcome to Hartwell. I could give you the grand tour, if you like."

Liv's stomach gave a loud rumble. She'd had a packet of peanuts for dinner the night before, not liking the thought of Gordo and his grubby-looking hands making the cheese toastie he'd offered. He'd then promptly fallen asleep at the bar. The only other customers were two men silently watch-ing a fishing show on a television mounted on the wall, so Liv had eaten the nuts, quaffed the glass of house wine Gor-do had poured and retreated to her bedroom.

"Breakfast first though," Celia said. "Cat food is in the cupboard to the far left next to the hot water urn. Do you like eggs? I could whip up a cheese and mushroom omelette."

"I don't want to be any bother." Liv's stomach gave an-other growl. She crossed to the cupboard. There was a red plastic bowl on the floor which she assumed was for the cat. Mr Tiddles wound himself around her legs as she scooped out some biscuits.

"No bother," Celia said. "I'm mostly doing prep for dinner tonight. We only have two guests staying at the moment, don't we, Simon?"

"Another due to arrive tomorrow, if the ferry is operating, and one coming in on the plane."

Liv looked around the clean but worn kitchen and wondered how the hotel could possibly keep operating if they had so few guests. From her observations, she could already see some improvements that could be made to make the hotel more appealing to an investor, but what would the point be if nobody wanted to stay there? From the glimpse she'd had of Agnes Island, it seemed a quiet, dreary place. Not the most appealing holiday destination. The hotel could be demolished, she supposed, but what would you build there instead? The land was probably worth nothing. Mr Tiddles was purring now as he chomped on his biscuits, reminding Liv that he was also an additional complication.

She leant on the kitchen counter and watched as Celia scraped sliced mushrooms into a pan and turned to crack eggs into a large bowl.

Simon was standing at the window. "Here's Ambrose. Better make that four omelettes."

Celia gave him a look. "What makes you assume I was making one for you?" There was a conveyor toaster on the counter and she put another two slices of bread in to toast.

Ambrose opened the door from outside a few seconds later. He toed off his gumboots and stepped inside. "Morning, smells good," he said, smiling at Celia. His face was transformed when he smiled, Liv thought, but then he caught sight of Liv and the smile dropped.

"Ah. Good morning, Olivia." He eyed her up and down and frowned. "Would you mind putting some clothes on? This is a hotel, not a guest house. It's not really appropriate to wander around public spaces in your pyjamas."

"We can hide her away back here, and then maybe smuggle her up the fire escape after breakfast," Celia said lightly. "Would you like an omelette?"

Liv straightened from where she'd been leaning. "I'll pop up and get dressed if there's time." She thought of the rickety fire escape. Meeting a guest on the stairway was preferable. She glanced pointedly down at Ambrose's feet, encased in thick beige socks. "Though, from my experience working in hospo, socks aren't really appropriate attire for a commercial kitchen."

When Liv came back down, Ambrose had gone. She sat with Celia and Simon and chatted over breakfast. Simon was lean and handsome, with a pierced ear, smooth sharp jawline and an ever-smiling mouth. He had come from Sydney to visit his sister and was helping out at the hotel while he was there, taking bookings and doing the cleaning. Celia came in each morning to make breakfast and prepare dinner for the nights the restaurant was open. She made sandwiches, cakes and a hot lunch too. The pub was popular with the locals, being the only place on the island for them to drink, especially in winter, with there not being as much work around, and the hotel's café was a popular meeting place during the day too.

Simon showed Liv around the hotel, starting upstairs with the guest rooms. The front section was currently the only part being used, with six rooms being in an acceptable condition for guests.

"It's two point five stars, at a push." He opened the door to one of the rooms that wasn't occupied. The room was much like Liv's own, slightly bigger, recently painted with reasonably new curtains. The bedding was bland and there were no embellishments aside from an ugly tulip print that hung above the bed.

"There's a shared bathroom in each wing of the rooms." He swung the door open with a flourish. "Two showers. Two separate toilets. The other wing is in a bit of a state and the bathroom's not operational at the moment."

"No en suites at all then?" Liv asked. Her mother had run a small bed and breakfast when Liv was growing up and even though they'd only had five rooms, each had its own bathroom at least.

"Well, there is one." Simon's eyes glinted. "You're in for a treat. Follow me."

Liv followed him, through a small communal living area, down a winding passage to the left wing of the hotel.

"These are the rooms that haven't been touched in literally decades. They're really a shambles. And this," he said, opening a door as though he were about to lead her into a grand ballroom, "is the honeymoon suite."

Liv stepped inside and drew in a breath. The wallpaper had once been red, it would seem, with a large embossed flower pattern, but had now faded to a mottled but still somehow garish pink. There was a large bed against the wall, possibly custom made as it was bigger than any bed Liv had seen, with a dirty satin headboard and bare kapok mattress. A huge, ugly painting of two dogs playing poker hung above the bed, which seemed an odd choice for a honeymoon suite and didn't really induce romantic vibes. Part of the ceiling was sagging above the bed. On the side wall, next to a decaying set of French doors, was an oak liquor cabinet. There were two moth-eaten armchairs positioned in front of the cabinet with an ugly, brown, spindly-legged table between them. The doors led out to a small balcony which didn't look stable enough to stand on. Liv could see there was a nice side view of the ocean though.

"Oh wow."

"Wow indeed. Isn't it fabulously awful? This is the bathroom." Simon opened a door. The en suite would have once been quite grand. There was a large cream-coloured shower unit that had probably been added sometime in the eighties. The floor was covered wall to door in threadbare peach carpet, and a large heart-shaped mirror, glass dotted with black chips and encrusted in seashells, held pride of place above the pedestal sink.

The rest of the rooms on the left wing were in an even worse state. Clearly the hotel didn't get enough guests for anyone to have bothered doing anything about them. Simon didn't take her into the wing where her room was. That had been used by the owner and staff for years, he explained, "which is why it's extra-hideously ugly."

"Wasn't the previous owner an artist?" Liv asked, as they went back downstairs to have a look at the bar.

"Laurie? Yes, he was supposedly an amazing painter. Apparently, he was always grouchy and a bit of a recluse. One of the local ladies ran the hotel back then and word is you'd hardly ever see Laurie, apart from when he'd come into the bar for his nightly tipple. There's a studio out the back where he painted, so I guess he spent most of his time there, but he'd been at a rest home on the mainland for a while before he died. Celia was basically running the place alone, before I got here, but Laurie didn't leave any instructions — or money — for any improvements." Simon pulled a set of keys from his pocket. "One of his paintings is in the Art Gallery of New South Wales actually. Did you not know him?"

"I … no. I went to his funeral, sort of by accident, and ended up in his will. It's a bit of a strange story."

He opened the door to the bar and they stepped through.

"Well, we must get into that over drinks. I'm not sure anyone would have gone up for the funeral, but I think the ferry was out that week in any case. Anyway, this was his hideaway…" His eyes swept around the bar. "It's not exactly a palace, is it?"

Liv wanted to ask him about Ambrose, and how he was related to Laurie. Surely if he was a grandson or great-nephew or something, Laurie would have left the hotel entirely to him? But if Simon was new here, maybe he wasn't the person to ask.

The bar was closed at this time of day and smelt of stale beer. It was cold and Liv shivered. Whatever sun there was couldn't get through the windows because of the caked-on salt. "Would anyone mind if I gave the windows a clean?"

Simon shrugged. "Go for gold. Gordo's meant to do that but his eyesight isn't so great these days. He's worked on the bar for as long as anyone can remember, lives in a caravan out the back of the hotel. I think he's supposed to take care of the gardens too, but he says he can't push the mower anymore 'cause of his back. I've done it a few times."

Liv could see weeds growing through the deck and wondered whether Gordo wasn't able to see those either.

She would clean the windows first, she decided, and make note of other small improvements they could make. Then she'd need to find Ambrose to talk about what they were going to do with this albatross of a hotel.

Chapter 6

The bar was surprisingly warm and busy when Liv came down that night after a super-quick shower. Gordo was at the long counter pouring beers for two grizzled-looking men in cable-knit jumpers. A younger couple sat at a table along the wall sharing a plate of nachos, her face grim as he watched the TV on the wall where a game of darts was playing.

A small group of older ladies sat at one of the tables by the window talking animatedly. They all wore purple ribbons clipped into their hair and a larger woman with glasses on a chain was taking notes in a spiral notebook. A squat older man with a few sparse tufts of white hair on his mottled head stood talking to Ambrose who was nodding politely and sipping on a beer. They all looked up as Liv entered, and the noise died down considerably. It was the first she'd seen of Ambrose since that morning and she pushed down her irritation, trying to look friendly.

"Well, speak of the devil," the old man said, and she noticed Ambrose blush. "You must be Olivia. I'm Howard, owner of the island's only taxi company."

Behind the counter where he was writing something down, Gordo snorted. "One shite Holden Sedan is not a company, you flamin' drongo," he called out. "I bet you never even passed your licence, the way you drive."

Howard glared at Gordo, pulling himself up to his full four foot four and puffing out his chest. "I'll have you know Sergeant Pinkle gave me my licence the day I turned fifteen, that's how good my driving is. I've been driving since I was eleven."

"Well, all that does is prove my bleedin' point," Gordo said. "You may as well have found it in a Weet-Bix packet. Tom would never pass you ..."

"Olivia, how lovely to meet you," one of the women interrupted, coming over and placing a hand lightly on Liv's forearm. She was tall and thin, with a stylish grey bob and smiling eyes, "Jackie Begal, I'm one of the community nurses and a member of the Pretty Pansies. Welcome to Aggie."

"Umm, thanks." Liv must have looked a little baffled because Jackie went on to explain. "We're a little group of ladies who help out where needed in the community. We also have an annual pansy-growing competition where a board of judges decides who has the winning crop. It's all good, clean fun."

"Well, I still think it's unfair that I can't join." Simon emerged from the kitchen with three plates of food. "I should *more* than qualify, although the clean part does put me off to be fair." Jackie laughed loudly, but a few of the other women looked a little taken aback. "Fish and chips, Liv?" Simon asked. "Twistie here brought in some blue cod caught today, so it couldn't get any fresher." He nodded his head towards one of the men at the bar, his eyes barely visible beneath a shock of long white hair, sideburns, droopy moustache and thick beard. He raised a hand in a sort of a wave and then turned back to his mate.

"That sounds fantastic, thanks, Simon," Liv said. "Have you eaten yet, Ambrose? Perhaps we could chat over dinner?"

They sat at one of the tables against the window where the rain had started again, tapping steadily against the glass. Outside only the odd light from a house or boat cut through the dark night. Liv sipped at her drink, trying to decide where to start.

"I think we probably got off on ..." she started, at the same time that Ambrose said, "I suppose you're going to want paying out, even though you didn't even know Laurie?"

They both looked at each other for a beat, Liv trying to read Ambrose, whose face was stony.

"You're clearly not the sort of woman who would want to ..."

"How exactly did you know Laurie?" She paused. "Would want to what?"

"Pardon?"

"The type of woman who would want to do what?" Liv could feel a bubble of anger forming in her chest. She took another, longer sip of her wine, trying to school her face.

"I simply meant that you don't seem like the type to want to live on a remote island." Ambrose fidgeted with his cutlery. "I mean, there's not much here for someone like you. There's no fancy clothing shops or beauty salon or rooftop bars. No shoe shop or jewellers or anything like that." He cleared his throat slightly. "So I'm assuming you're not planning on staying? I would need to buy you out, I suppose, if you intend to accept your half of the inheritance?"

Liv curled her fist under the table and took a few breaths in through her nose as she tried to gather her thoughts. Ambrose clearly had an impression of her, and it wasn't great. But the fact was, she did need to stay, at least for a bit, until all the media attention died down.

And *if* she planned to take her half? Why shouldn't she? Except that maybe he was right. Maybe she didn't really deserve to take anything. Maybe Ambrose was more entitled to the hotel? She vaguely remembered him mentioning spending time here as a child.

"Are you related to Mr Lloyd then?" she asked. Was Ambrose blushing again? She leant back in her chair to study him. He seemed less assured than she had thought. He slugged a mouthful of beer and then wiped at his mouth.

"I was good friends with his grandson Mike," he said. "I spent most of my summer holidays here as a boy."

"So why didn't Mike get all this?" Liv waved her arm vaguely around the room, almost hitting Simon in the nuts as he arrived with their meals. "Shit, sorry, Simon."

"Mike died a few years ago in a motorbike accident," Ambrose said quietly, and Liv felt like a right bitch.

"Sorry," she muttered again. "Did he not have any other relatives then, Laurie? Did Mike have any kids?"

Ambrose's face was pink again. He blushed easily.

"I'm not really sure," he admitted. "Mike and I lost touch in high school. He was an only child, never knew his father and I heard his mother died before the accident. I think he was married, or had been, but I don't know if he had any children, I'm guessing not."

"I see." Liv chewed on one of her fries, thinking. Ambrose clearly had more claim to the inheritance than her, but it was a tenuous connection if he hadn't seen Laurie's grandson since he was what — twelve? Thirteen? Plus, she really didn't have anywhere else to go. But he had mentioned paying her out. Did that mean he planned to stay here? "Look, I have no idea what a place like this is worth, but in the state it's in, I doubt we'd get a buyer, don't you? I think the best thing we can probably do is get the hotel as functioning as possible, while spending as little as possible to do it, and then put it on the market," she said. "Or you buy me out and take custody of Mr Tiddles."

"I do want it," he said. "But I don't have the money to pay you out. And I agree, it needs some work. You might be surprised, but I remember it being a lot busier on Aggie when I was a kid. So I suggest we get it back to its original condition where we can and try to get it making some money to fund the renovations. Then we can look at selling, or hopefully by then I can buy your half."

"It's a deal."

They both set upon their fish and chips, and when Ambrose was done he left with a curt goodnight. Liv sat looking out the newly clean windows, wondering how long she could bear to stay here. Ambrose might think she was a high-maintenance city girl, but he was wrong. She knew how to work hard, and she didn't need much. Shoes and makeup and designer labels she could live without, but right now she was lonely.

There was a scratching sound and then scrabbling until Mr Tiddles was perched up on the seat Ambrose had vacated. He eyed her steadily until she put a small piece of blue cod on the table in front of him.

"I guess it's you and me then," Liv sighed.

Chapter 7

Ambrose woke up early like always and lay in bed listening to the sound of the waves rolling and crashing down on the shore, soothing and familiar.

He and Mike had spent hours exploring the beach down by the ferry dock, riding bikes around the island, climbing the lighthouse, looking for kiwi and, best of all, looking for treasure with maps Laurie had hand-drawn for them.

Most of the islanders had found Laurie grumpy and rude, but Mike and Ambrose knew a different side to him. Ambrose had loved sneaking into his studio to watch him paint and he had been unexpectedly patient with the boys and their endless questions.

Ambrose had so many great memories here. So much of his childhood had been boarding school and nannies and parents, who it had seemed never really wanted a child. But Aggie had been his chance to run wild and free with Mike and Glenn, and even Tom at the start, feeling like he fit in and had a place he belonged.

A car was coming slowly up the gravel road. Howie, he thought, judging by its lack of speed. It was too early for the ferry and he wondered if the sea plane had come, bringing one of their guests. He remembered how Laurie would let him and Mike drive the old golf buggy down to the ferry sometimes to pick up passengers, how they would pass Howie on the main road, going so slowly that Mike could beat him running down the strip even with Howie getting a head start.

He thought about Olivia in the next room, with her long blonde hair and diamond earrings and he wondered if he could bring himself to ask his parents for a loan to pay her out and keep the hotel. Then he could restore it back to how it had been when he was a kid, standing proud on the hill, a grand old lady in red. He stretched, his long legs poking out the end of the bed, the morning air frigid against his feet. Maybe they should start with the heating, he thought with a grimace.

By the time Ambrose had dressed and made his way downstairs, Howie had pulled up outside the front entrance and a slight man in a flamboyant purple suit was stepping out, a leather satchel over his shoulder. He had thick-rimmed scarlet glasses and a Hercule Poirot moustache. Howie lifted out a Louis Vuitton suitcase from the boot, struggling under its weight.

"There you go, Mr Price, safe and sound." He thumped it down on the doorstep.

"And in under an hour no less," the man said wryly, looking up at the hotel. "Good grief, how has this place not been condemned yet?" He handed Howie some cash and then started to make his way up the steps as Olivia appeared from around the back of the hotel, wrapped up in a large fur jacket, covered in cobwebs.

"Sweetheart, you have a large black spider on your shoulder," the man pointed out, and Ambrose forced himself to stay calm as she casually flicked it off onto the deck. He watched it warily until it disappeared down a crack.

"Thanks," she said, smiling, then not, as she turned to him. "Is there a key for the old stone building out back?" she asked. "I was hoping to find a ladder in there."

"I think I can help," the man said. "I'm Malcolm Price, Mr Lloyd's agent. And that building, or what's in it, is exactly why I'm here."

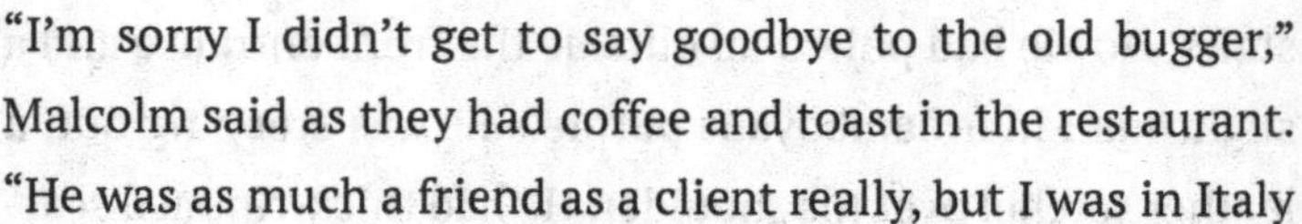

"I'm sorry I didn't get to say goodbye to the old bugger," Malcolm said as they had coffee and toast in the restaurant. "He was as much a friend as a client really, but I was in Italy when I heard and I knew there was no point coming back. It's a shame he didn't get to do the lap of the island."

"The lap?" Ambrose asked, distracted. Olivia had taken off her jacket and her pink top was rather fitted. He tried not to notice how low cut it was.

"It's an old tradition," Malcolm said. "Nigel gives them a scenic flight of the island as a final farewell. Laurie would have liked that."

"I read he was quite famous as a painter," Olivia said. "I saw some of his work when I googled him. It's lovely."

"He was incredible." Malcolm sipped his green tea. "And his best work has never been seen. Hence my visit." He fished in his jacket pocket and produced a letter that he placed on the table. Ambrose looked over at Olivia who nodded at him, so he picked it up and read out loud.

Malcolm, old chap, you will be pleased to know the time has come. Ida has gone, and hopefully I'll be soon to follow. I know how much you wanted to exhibit the paintings and I'm sorry to have kept them from you, but I made a promise, and I kept it. Now, it no longer matters, so show them to whomever you want, hang them up and let them say what they will. Exhibit them on the island though. Make the punters come to me.

Except not the nude. That one is going to stay under wraps, sorry.

The paintings are in the studio, ready to go. There's also a little something for you in the tin — think of me when you use it. Burn the rest of the contents, will you? They mean nothing to anyone else.

Now Mike's gone, I've left the hotel to whomever can be arsed to show up to the funeral. Maybe that's only you? Although I doubt you'll want it. I know how much you hate that ferry trip. Whoever gets it, good luck to them. They might find the same peace I did on Aggie, they might want to burn the old girl down. I don't care. Please make sure Mr Tiddles is looked after though, will you?

You've been a good agent and a better friend and I thank you for that.

Yours,
Lawrence Lloyd

"I have no idea how many pieces of art are out there," Malcolm said. "But I've started putting the word out and I'd like to exhibit them as soon as I can." He looked around the room. "I think the place may need a little more work than I anticipated though." He set down his cup and reached into his bag, pulling out some forms. "The good news is, there's money set aside to get the exhibition ready and we may be able to use some of that on the hotel. People are going to need somewhere to sleep, and between this dump and the camping ground, you're slightly in the lead."

Olivia laughed. She had a cute laugh, Ambrose thought.

"So all the art is in the studio out back? I wonder why he didn't paint anything for the hotel? The artwork in here is atrocious."

"He always did have a strange sense of humour." Malcolm looked around at the framed posters hanging on the walls.

"Well, I love that one." Ambrose pointed to a poster of a cheesy-looking pirate at the helm of a ship. "I was here when they filmed that movie. Tad Chadwick played the lead and he was my hero."

Olivia's head shot up from where she had been reading the letter again.

"Tad Chadwick was here?"

Too late, Ambrose remembered that Olivia knew Tad's son, Sean Anthony. Rather too well, if the reports were to be believed. And he was married with kids. Ambrose and Olivia's eyes met across the table and an awkward moment passed between them.

"He's acting royalty, isn't he? Pity he retired," Malcolm said, oblivious. "I loved him in that bank robber movie."

"He signed my T-shirt," Ambrose said. "But the maid put it through the wash."

"Shame, it would probably be worth a fair bit now ..." But Ambrose would never have sold it. "Speaking of which..."

Malcolm pulled a key from his top pocket, "...let's go and open this studio."

The problem arose when they got inside.

The studio itself was a large stone barn structure, with exposed beams and a mezzanine floor that ran along the back and sides in a C formation with a rickety stairwell up the wall nearest the door. Only one light seemed to be working and dust motes swam around the thin stream of light it gave off. The place was filthy, everything covered in a layer of grime and the floor deep with sand, leaves and God knows what else. There were rags and paint tubes and old canvases stacked up against the wall and in one corner a tarp covered something. The whole thing smelt of mould and decay.

The small room under the overhang was the room Laurie used as an office and there was a grimy bathroom next to it, the taps bleeding rust into the pedestal sink.

It looked nothing like Ambrose remembered it. Presumably the locked office was where the artwork was kept and he hoped it was in a better state than the rest of the building. Malcolm inserted the old-style key into the large rusty lock, only to have it snap off when he tried to turn it. They all stood and looked as he held the end of the key up in shock.

"Well, bugger," Malcolm said. "That wasn't in the plan." He peered down at the keyhole in dismay. "I don't suppose there's a locksmith on Aggie?"

"I'll go and ask Gordo," Ambrose offered, keen to get away from all the cobwebs.

"Ask him if there's a pest exterminator too, will you?" Olivia called after him. "It looks like there might be something living up in the rafters."

He was only walking so fast because it was cold, he told himself.

Chapter 8

The ferry had apparently been and there was a large box on the front counter with Liv's name on it when she got back to the front desk. A woman was also checking in, dressed in dark leggings and wearing a beanie, a pair of dark sunglasses perched on top of it. Simon gave her a smile as he handed over a key.

"There you go, Ms Hemingway, room eight, up the stairs to your left."

"I hope the room has good light." The woman picked up her luggage; a large carpet bag type thing and a case. "I'm a writer, you see. It's very important."

"Best view in the house," Simon said with a smile. If Liv's recollection was correct, room eight was a dingy room next to the bathroom with one window but good proximity to the coffee-making station.

Ms Hemingway looked around the shabby lobby with pursed lips. "Is there no elevator?"

"I'm afraid not." Liv stepped forward. The woman was

probably in her early thirties, but she could have a hidden health condition so Liv wasn't going to be too quick to judge. "These old hotels, you know. Do you need a hand with your bags?"

"No, no, I can manage." She paused to look at the picture hanging at the bottom of the stairway. It showed a large pelican wearing a captain's hat on a small ferry. "I'm writing a book about birds, you know." She leant closer as if examining the print in detail.

"Well, you won't find many pelicans around this neck of the woods, unless it's a tourist from Australia," Simon said.

"No, no, I know that of course. I was just wondering who the artist was."

"Clipart, I imagine."

"Is it? Well, I know nothing about art, as you can tell. Absolutely nothing." She looked intently at Liv's face. "You look familiar. Were you that daft girl who turned down Connor Reed?" She gave Liv a sympathetic pat on her arm. "I hear he's dating a model now."

Simon and Liv watched as their guest mounted the stairs. "How exciting, a writer on Aggie." Simon pushed the box on the counter forward. "Are you going to open that? Did you order something online?"

"I didn't." Liv recognised her mother's neat block writing under the courier label. She'd sent Deirdre a text after she'd arrived on Agnes Island to say she'd got there safely and that the hotel needed a lot of work. Deirdre hadn't replied and, to be honest, Liv had no idea how her mother felt about the whole inheritance thing.

"Scissors?" Simon handed her a pair and she slit the tape on the top.

There was a neatly folded letter, on top of two large bottles of bleach, a roll of rubbish bags and a five-litre container of industrial Spray and Wipe. A bottle of multivitamins was wedged down the side, along with a massive packet of rubber gloves.

Simon peered into the box. "Crikey. Are you planning on killing someone?"

Ambrose's glum face flashed before Liv's eyes. "I could be persuaded."

"Let me know if you need help hiding the body. We could do with a bit of excitement around here."

Liv unfolded the letter.

Dear Livvy,

I hope this finds you well and you're settling into island life. I can't imagine what that must be like. You're such a brave girl.

Anyway, the thought of that run-down hotel has me awake worrying. I hope you will use the enclosed products to ensure you have healthy and hygienic surroundings. The bleach can be diluted one part to five parts of water. I would have liked to send you a bag of oranges but wasn't sure how long the courier would take to get to you so the vitamin tablets will have to suffice.

All my love,
Mum

"My mother." Liv folded the letter back up and put it into the box.

"Interesting care package," Simon said. "When I was at boarding school, my father once sent me a chocolate cake from a local bakery. It had 'Happy birthday' iced on it, and it wasn't even my birthday, I told the other boys it was though."

Ambrose came through the bar door and stopped short when he saw them.

"No locksmith on Aggie," he said to Liv. "We could get one over from the mainland but they wouldn't arrive until the next ferry, which is two days away. Gordo suggested we call Chipper, the local handyman." He turned to Simon. "Do we have his number?"

Simon flipped an old Rolodex on the counter to the Cs. "Do we have a surname, perchance, or is this person known purely as Chipper — rather like Beyonce?"

"I'm not sure anyone has surnames around here," Ambrose said.

"We could have a talk to this Chipper bloke about doing some renovations." Liv ran her hand over the stair railing.

"I'd love to see this restored back to its original condition, and I'm scared someone's going to pull it down with them."

Ambrose nodded in rare agreement. "We need to get a move on those unused rooms too, if we're going to host an art exhibition."

"Ooh, an art exhibition?" Simon ripped off the sheet of paper he had written the number for Chipper on and handed it to Ambrose. "How very city of us."

"That's if we can unlock the room that holds Laurie's paintings." Ambrose took his phone out of his pocket. "I can't believe such a valuable collection has been sitting in that shed mouldering away all this time."

The stairs creaked and the guest, Ms Hemingway, appeared at the top.

"I was wondering what the meal arrangements were?" she asked.

"I'll try to get hold of Chipper," Ambrose said, leaving Liv to deal with their guest.

Malcolm had decided that Laurie's old studio building was the only place on Agnes Island they could hold the exhibition. There was a community hall, which doubled as the building the small primary school used for indoor activities and assemblies, but it wasn't really suitable for an exhibition of that calibre, and long term Malcolm was hoping they'd have a permanent exhibition of Laurie's work, and where better than the space he'd created his paintings. It was only fitting.

"The old building has terrible lighting." Malcolm forked up a piece of Celia's chocolate cake while he and Liv waited for Chipper to turn up. "It used to be a stable back in the day. I really don't know how he painted under such barbaric conditions. I certainly couldn't, but the man was a genius. The upside is, it's the ideal space to start from scratch. I'm thinking rustic, exposed walls, keep the beams, that kind of thing." He waved his arms effusively.

"I'm not sure whether we've got the right people on the island for a project like that," Liv said. "You'll need builders? Electricians?"

"Specialty lighting experts, an experienced builder, proper temperature control. I've got connections through several of the galleries I've worked with." Malcolm took a sip of his tea. "I guess that means I'll have to oversee everything, which will mean staying on the island." He didn't look thrilled at the thought. "Don't worry, I'll sort that side of things. You just have to make sure there are as many rooms available in the hotel as possible."

"Sounds easy," Liv said wryly. "How long do we have?"

"Even with great efficiency it will take around three months to organise. We'll want the weather to be a bit more stable and I might have to hire some charter boats that can ferry people over and back for the opening day. It won't be possible for everyone to stay, though why they'd want to brave a double crossing in one day is beyond me."

When Ambrose turned up with the handyman in tow, Malcolm excused himself to call a few people to get things in motion. Liv recognised Chipper as half of the darts-watching couple from a few nights previously. He was a morose-looking man with thinning hair and a large beak-like nose, so tall that he stooped when he walked. They crossed to the studio, the uneven stone path slippery under their feet. Another job that would need to be sorted. The place was really overgrown and a bit of simple landscaping would make all the difference. Liv pushed down the feeling of overwhelm.

Chipper scratched the side of his nose as he peered into the lock.

"Looks like there's something blocking it," he said.

"It's a key," Ambrose said. Liv thought he showed a remarkable amount of patience, considering he'd already explained the situation. "Do you think you can open the door?"

"Hard to say. It's one of them old locks. I might have to take the door off its hinges."

"When do you think you'd be able to do that?"

"Well, it's also one of them old kinds of security doors. You'll be best getting a locksmith in, mate."

"Right. So we'll need to get someone over on the ferry." Ambrose ran a hand through his hair, which flopped back a bit messily afterwards. Liv thought it made him look softer and not so grumpy, even though the frown was back on his face. "I don't suppose there's anyone else on Aggie that could do it?"

"Nope, I'm your man," Chipper said. Though he clearly wasn't. "Me and the missus moved here two years ago, which was just as well since Jack, the only builder on the island, retired to Nelson. No job is too big or too small."

"Except this one?"

Liv interjected. "We may have some renovation work for you if you're interested?" She didn't have the utmost confidence, but they were short of options, and it seemed like they'd need to get moving on the project as soon as possible.

There was a scuttling sound from the rafters above them, a rat perhaps?

"Let's talk about it back at the hotel," Ambrose said. "We can show you what needs doing, and It's bloody freezing in here."

"I wouldn't mind some fish and chips and a beer." Chipper bent slightly as they exited the studio. "Greta hasn't been doing much cooking this week — busy with school stuff." Liv pulled the door shut behind them and they followed Ambrose, who was striding back down the stone path like there was a pack of wolves snapping at his heels.

Chapter 9

Liv's clothes and boots were covered in a layer of dust and her hair was grey with spiderwebs by the time she came in for the day. She hadn't made as much headway as she would have liked in the studio, but she had managed to clear out one corner and uncovered the tarp to discover an old golf cart and several bicycles as well as a shovel, broom, some gardening tools and an old wooden ladder. One of the bikes was in pretty good condition, only needing a bit of grease on the chain and the back tyre pumped up, and Liv thought she might take it down in the morning to the little gas station in town by the ferry wharf and see if she could get it rideable.

She really wanted to wash her hair, but settled for giving it a thorough brush instead, too scared of Ambrose's wrath. She'd brought what she thought would be suitable clothes for the island, but as she pulled on her Calvin Klein jeans and a warm jumper, she surveyed the rest of her clothes. They were all too fancy, especially for mucking out or cleaning.

She wished she had packed some track pants or something a little more casual.

Her bank account was in dire straits. There was no budget for new clothes. Or anything really. She rang her mum. One of the only benefits of her mother's struggling mental health was that she knew she would be home. She answered on the third ring and her voice was enough to make Liv feel a little choked up.

"Hi, Mum, just me," she said, trying to sound upbeat.

"Livvy, darling, how are you? I was just thinking of you. I forgot to add the bed bug bombs into your package so I'm going to try to get a courier pick-up next week."

"Thanks, but you don't need to do that, we've had no sign of any bugs anyway."

"Well, if you do, the freezer is the best way to kill them," her mum said. Liv could hear her spraying something and then a squeaking noise like a cloth on glass. "Are you keeping warm, hun?"

"I'm okay. I was wondering though if you might be able to sell my car?" There was silence on the other end. Liv knew her mum would not like dealing with strangers coming to look at it.

"Won't you need it when you come back?" her mum asked. "You are coming back, aren't you, Liv?"

"Yes, of course, I was just thinking I might need ..." Liv trailed off. She *would* need her car when she left here. But if she told her mum she needed the money, she would try to offer her a loan, and Liv knew money was tight. She would just have to make things stretch. "Actually, Mum, never mind, I was just thinking it was sitting there unused, but you're right, I will need it soon."

"Well, I'm sure things will die down soon enough with the Connor thing." Her mum was running water now. Probably cleaning the shower. "Although there was an interview in one of the magazines saying you had blindsided him and the heartbreak was putting him off his game. Plus there was a small mention of you in the sports section on Sunday after they lost again. So silly."

"I suppose I'm still to blame?" Liv sighed.

"They'll forget you soon enough," her mum said firmly. "Now, how is everything else? Tell me all about the island."

Liv tried to think of something positive to tell her. "Well, it's very quiet, and the view is amazing," she said.

"And how are you getting on with the other owner — Mr McCafferty, isn't it?"

"Ambrose." Liv pulled on her sneakers. "I don't think he's very happy that I'm here."

"What do you mean? With all your expertise helping me run this place, I'd have thought you'd be a godsend."

"A bed and breakfast is a little bit different though, isn't it?"

"Well, the principle is the same. He's lucky to have you."

"I'll point that out to him. Anyway, how are you?"

"Oh, I'm fine. Same old four walls, but I rather miss having you around."

Liv smiled. "I miss you too. I'd better go and get some dinner, but I'll talk to you soon?"

"All right, love you, Liv."

"Love you too, Mum."

In the bar, the TV was on the sports channel again, and it was pretty crowded. Liv scanned the room. Malcolm sat at a table alone, nursing a dark amber-coloured drink, engrossed in a Dick Francis novel. She noted Chipper was now drinking with the two fishermen from last night and another guy who looked like the ferry captain. They were at a table with Jackie and another lady, who both wore All Blacks scarfs. The two men were scowling as they all looked over, but Jackie gave her a wave.

She'd almost forgotten about Connor the last few days, but a quick glance at the TV reminded her that tonight was one of their big games. Maybe she could take a meal back to her room, she thought. The last thing she wanted to do was sit and watch the match.

"Hello, again," a man called from behind her, and she turned to find the big bear-like guy from the ferry dock coming in the door with a plastic container in his large hands. "I'm Glenn Moa. I'm here to drop off the pies. Ambrose suggested I come up and have dinner with him, so I thought I'd

..." He laughed suddenly, deep and rumbling. "I was going to say kill two birds with one stone." He smiled, showing all his straight, even teeth. "Except I would never." He gave someone a funny little wave behind her. "Kill birds, that is. I love birds," he told Liv.

"Speaking of loving birds ..." Simon came up to take the container from Glenn. "... and we're clearly not talking about me, we have a lady here writing a book about them. I'm sure she'd be keen for a late-night outing with you."

Glenn blushed a deep red from the neck up. "I meant the vertebrates with feathers," he said, "not birds as in ... I'm the local kiwi guide if you ever want to see one," he offered Liv.

Simon laughed. "I'm only teasing, big guy — ah, here she is."

Their most recent guest was coming into the bar, her hair and makeup done and wearing a navy wool dress. Someone whistled.

"Don't be ridiculous, you old coot," Gordo said. "She's half your age and then some." Howie, who had been the whistler and was sitting by an old jukebox, gave him the finger.

"Ms Hemingway," Simon called. The room was noisy and Ms Hemingway didn't hear so he waved to get her attention. "We must stop calling you Ms Hemingway," he said as she came over. "It makes you sound like a character in a Dickens story."

"Yes, um, Julia is fine," she mumbled.

Liv invited Julia to join them. Glenn offered to get a round of drinks and went to the counter, so Liv indicated a table and she and Julia sat to wait.

"Can I put in a meal order for you two?" Simon asked. "Let's see, we've got venison burgers, fish and chips or a mushroom risotto and now — also pies." He opened up one corner of the container and peeked in. "Looks like mince."

"Venison mince," Glenn said, coming back with two handles of beer, Liv's wine, a gin and tonic for Julia and a glass of what looked like orange juice that he handed over to Howie at the adjacent table. "I make all my own pies and sausages." He put down the drinks and pulled out a chair. "The New Zealand Game Animal Council contract me to keep the deer under control, so I do all my own butchering and make use of the meat."

"Fantastic, bet they're popular," Liv said.

Simon gave a funny snort. "Most people love them." He placed one hand on his hip. "You might have noticed though, Glenn, that I'm not like the other men on Aggie."

Glenn went red again, his Adam's apple visible as he gulped down his beer.

"I'm a vegetarian." Simon gave an exaggerated wink.

Glenn put down his beer and looked up at Simon who was grinning widely. "You should know better than to judge a book by its cover, love," he said quietly. "I'm not like all the other men either, and I'll have the risotto, thanks, even though I'm not a vegetarian."

Simon took a step back in surprise. This time it was

him blushing and Liv took a sip of her wine to stop herself laughing.

"I'll have the same," she said. Julia ordered the fish and chips.

Glenn called out to someone behind them. "I've got your beer, mate, what are you eating?"

"Cheers, Glenn. I'll take a pie, thanks, Simon," Ambrose called back as he crossed the room towards them. He was smiling again, Liv noted, his hair wet. Unlike her, he'd clearly had time to shower and he hadn't even helped in the studio. She patted her own ponytail self-consciously, wondering if she'd missed any cobwebs, then laughed at the thought of a spider scuttling out as Ambrose took a seat.

"Something funny?" he asked, back to scowling. "Or are you just happy we're losing the game?"

"Yeah, I don't know what you've got to laugh about," a man called out. It was one of the fishermen. "If it wasn't for you we'd be taking home the cup, and Connor Reed would be a hero instead of a laughing stock."

It felt like the whole bar went quiet. Liv wasn't sure what to say or where to look, but when her eyes caught on Ambrose, she was shocked to see he looked smug, even gleeful, a smirk on his face. She looked away, her stomach knotting and her whole body vibrating with the need to flee.

"That's enough, Morris," Jackie said loudly. "It's not poor Olivia's fault Connor isn't performing. She can hardly be blamed for every crap game he plays from now on, can she?"

"Don't listen to him, Liv." Celia came over to take the pies from Simon, who was still looking a little wide-eyed at Glenn. "He's just mad 'cause he lost a bet with Puff."

"Keep that up, Morris, and I'll put you on the no-serve list with Howie," Gordo said, writing something down in a large ledger. "And don't think I didn't see you give Howie that drink, Glenn."

Glenn laughed and Simon took the opportunity to turn back to the kitchen.

"I'll get those orders in." He gave Liv a sad smile.

"Actually, would you mind if I took mine to go?" she asked quietly. "I'm quite tired, so I might eat in my room." She pushed her chair back from the table and stood, avoiding looking at Ambrose. "Thanks for the drink, Glenn, if you'll all excuse me."

"No problem," Simon said. "I'll bring it up, yeah?"

Liv took a long hot shower. She shampooed her hair twice and conditioned it. Fuck Ambrose, she thought, as the water washed away her tears.

Chapter 10

Ambrose got up early the next morning, planning to go for a run down to the beach. He'd had a bad night's sleep, tossing and turning and thinking about all the things that needed to be arranged for the hotel and the exhibition.

The locksmith was sorted and they'd secured Chipper for renovations, but there was so much else that needed doing. He'd need to get an evaluation on the hotel once it was done up. They'd need new bedding once the neglected wing was renovated, new beds too probably, and other bits and pieces that might need to come from the mainland. The whole outside of the hotel needed sanding and painting and it would all need to be paid for somehow.

And then there was the land. It was severely overgrown and although Simon had mowed the lawn and trimmed back the bushes out front, the back was a jungle. There'd once been a hot tub back there, he remembered, which sat on a bed of smooth river pebbles, enclosed in a little grotto. Laurie had often sent the boys to collect driftwood to burn to warm up the rain water supplied by a small tank beside it. Then Laurie would strip naked and put on music and soak in the tub, singing loudly and out of tune. There was no sign of it now, the bush overtaking the back lawn.

As he stepped out on the veranda with a handful of sunflower seeds, calling out for Lester, a movement caught his eye. Olivia emerged from the back building, wheeling an old bike. She was in leggings and a tight long-sleeve top, her toned stomach slightly visible. He watched her set off down the hill, shoulders hunched, the bike squeaking with every wheel rotation, hair in that long ponytail, bouncing with each step. He watched her until she was on the flat and a loud squawk made him jump. Lester was there, ready for his seeds, and Ambrose held out his hand, pleased to have his thoughts taken away from Olivia for a moment.

Things on the island were the same and yet different from when he was here all those years ago. Some of the faces were the same, like Glenn and Tom who had grown up here, attending the local school but befriending Ambrose and Mike, probably as a novelty to start, or to make up numbers on their sports teams.

The school was still the same. Three wooden rooms in a long row, one used as an office and staffroom, the others classrooms for the small group of kids that lived here. It went up to year eight, so kids from ages five to twelve shared the space along with the teachers. After that most of the kids went to the mainland to boarding school, or were homeschooled.

There was no school pool. The kids learnt to swim in the ocean. The large field out front was used for rugby, soccer and hockey. But they had a basketball or netball court now, and a small greenhouse and garden stood where there had once been nothing but scrub.

There was a small office in town now too, to buy the ferry tickets and where tourists could book fishing trips and whale-watching tours as well.

The town library had been extended and there was now a small cinema attached to the one side of the post office. The airstrip was finally signposted, and the old police hut had been upgraded to a proper building next to the medical centre.

The shops hadn't changed much. There was the local dairy, a second-hand shop for clothes and bric-a-brac, and a garage where they also sold bait and fishing gear. Anything else had to come from the mainland.

Down the hill Olivia was now riding the bike along the main street, her long legs pumping the pedals, ponytail flying. Ambrose sighed, deciding against running, and headed back inside to the office to try to make sense of Laurie's books.

Laurie had not been a fan of technology it would seem. Almost all his hotel check-ins were done manually. There were boxes and boxes of ledgers in the small office off the reception area, dating back years and stacked in no logical order. There were folders of receipts, tax forms and scraps of paper with phone numbers. Even the cash register at the bar was old-fashioned, with Gordo scribbling away in a black leatherbound book when guests had no cash. Ambrose had been trying for weeks to make some sort of sense of any of it. It was amazing there hadn't been issues with the tax department.

There was a safe, he had discovered, set into a wall under the desk, and it had a small amount of cash in it, less than a thousand, and a bank account that no one seemed to use, with three hundred and sixty-eight dollars in it, most of it from accrued interest.

Celia had told him that most people paid cash for their room when they arrived, but the majority of the money the hotel earned was from the bar and restaurant. She had set up a new account for that when she started working there. That at least seemed to be organised and was making enough to pay staff wages. But it wasn't making any significant profit as far as he could see, once she'd purchased alcohol and food ingredients every fortnight or so, which came on the ferry from the mainland.

He transferred some of his own money into the account so he could pay the landline phone bill, and put in an order for an eftpos machine, then made a call about someone coming over to look at the internet and computer system, which needed a drastic overhaul. It all seemed a bit overwhelming, there was so much to do and sort out.

Once his little apartment sold, he'd have some idea how much more he needed to pay out Olivia. Ambrose was an optimist though. If they could get the hotel ready for the exhibition, people would come to the island to see Laurie's work, surely? And they would stay and see the beauty of the place, like he did.

The front door banged and Ambrose jumped. When he put his head out the door, no one was around. He rubbed at his temples, trying to decide what else needed doing and where to start. Coffee, he decided.

He brewed a cup and then went out to the studio to see what progress Olivia had made. He felt a tiny bit guilty that he was leaving the cleaning up to her, but he had so much other stuff to do, and she hadn't even asked about the running of the hotel. Her focus seemed to be solely on getting the place physically ready for sale. He still had hope that he could take over her share, so he wanted to make sure systems were in place to make the hotel function optimally.

There was a shrill shriek from inside the studio as he reached out to open the door and he may have let out a small noise himself. The door swung open and a woman appeared, flailing her arms about. It was Julia, the guest who had joined him and Glenn for dinner last night.

"What's wrong?" he asked and she shrieked again, clutching at her chest.

"My God, you scared me," she said. "First something came flapping at me in there, and then you, sneaking up on me."

Ambrose wasn't sure what to make of that. "What were you doing in the studio?"

"What? Yes, umm, I was looking for ... owls." She rubbed her nose. "Research, for my book."

"Owls," Ambrose repeated. "Like morepork you mean?"

"More what?" Julia dusted down the pants of her leggings that were covered in dust.

"Morepork," Ambrose repeated, peering over her shoulder to look through the open door. "Ruru? I'm not sure if we have any on Agnes Island actually. But Glenn would know."

"Ah, yes, ruru," Julia said. "I'm so used to calling them by their scientific name, I didn't register when you said morepork." She laughed lightly. "Well, I'd better get on with the writing, it's a very intense process, you know."

"Māori name," Ambrose corrected, but she was already off down the path towards the hotel.

It seemed a little odd, Ambrose thought, stepping through the door and reaching gingerly for the light switch. He was fairly sure morepork didn't live in manmade structures.

The studio looked the same, except possibly a little less dusty and one large section had been swept clean, a stack of leaves and debris in the corner, some tools leaning against the wall where a ladder rested. Ambrose did a tentative lap around, looking for who knows what, but there was nothing that came flapping out at him. The tarp had been shifted and he held one corner carefully with his fingertips and then lifted it up. The old golf buggy was under it, making Ambrose smile.

"It doesn't start," Olivia called from outside the open doorway and Ambrose only narrowly refrained from shrieking. "Have you come to help?" There was something in her tone that made him look up. She was angry, he realised. At him, if he had to guess.

"No, I was just checking on things," he said, about to explain about Julia.

"Things?" Olivia repeated. "As in, how much I've managed to get done? I'm not a bloody machine, you know. There's only me here doing it."

"Okay, okay, calm down." Ambrose realised his error the minute he said it. Rookie mistake. Never, ever tell a woman to calm down. "I'll see if I can get you some help," he said quickly.

"Big of you," she said sarcastically, getting back on the bike she was gripping and taking off.

Chapter 11

Liv guided the bike over deep ruts and bumps, down the hill into town, seething. How dare Ambrose check up on her, when he's been doing what? Avoiding any heavy work, that's what it seemed like. Acting like she had no claim to the hotel. Poking away in the office, making phone calls on his mobile phone. How difficult could it be to locate a locksmith to come over to the island? He was the most infuriating man she'd ever met. Give or take.

When she'd called in to the garage earlier she'd noticed a small second-hand shop next to the community hall. It had been closed but the sign suggested that it would be open in the afternoon. Liv pulled up outside now, leant the bike against an exterior wall and unhooked the bungee cord that held the bulging rubbish sack to the bike carrier and hoisted it over her shoulder.

She was surprised to see Bridie Allen, proprietor of the local store whom she'd met on her first day on the island, behind the counter.

"Hello, love, how are you getting on?" Bridie said. "What have you got there for me?"

"I was hoping to swap some of the clothes I brought over for something a bit more practical for the island." Liv dumped the bag onto the counter and Bridie rifled through it, pulling out clothes and sorting them into piles on the counter. "We're doing some renovations to the hotel. Can I have a look around at what you've got?"

"Of course, love." Bridie pulled out a pair of strappy pumps and held them up. "Goodness, are these Ferragamo? I think we could do a bit of a deal."

Liv selected a couple of hoodies and thermal tops, track pants, a thick cable-knit jumper and a pair of overalls with a slightly fishy odour. She eyed up the work socks, feeling a little queasy about used footwear.

"We have new socks at the store," Bridie said. "Underwear too and gumboots. Anything else you'll need to take a trip over to the city."

Liv took her purchases to the counter and Bridie bagged them up. At the last minute, Liv added a fluffy pink cushion to the pile. It would cheer her room up a little.

"Come back any time." Bridie glanced at her watch. "I'm sure we owe you a bit more than what you've taken away." She left the piles of clothes on the counter and followed Liv outside, locking the door behind them. "I'd better get over and open the booking office before the boat comes in."

"Is there no one at the store?" Liv had been hoping to get

a few things to supplement the restaurant meals she'd been eating. Celia had said she was welcome to use the kitchen, and there was also a small kitchenette that Laurie had used, on the opposite side of the corridor to her room.

"It'll be open again after three, when the ferry's gone. You can pop back then or do an online order."

"Really? An online order?" The internet had been a bit patchy on the island so far.

"Yes, you call me up on the telephone line and I'll get it ready for you," Bridie cackled. "We can even get Howie to drop it off, as long as it's not urgent."

There was a police cruiser parked outside when Liv arrived back. A large shaggy dog had its nose stuck through a gap in the window, its tongue lolling and breath fogging the glass. Inside the hotel, the man who had shared the outdoor space with Liv on the ferry was talking to Simon.

"Ah, here she is now," Simon said. "Tom, this is Olivia Peterson. Tom Harris, the one and only local copper."

"Liv," she said, holding out a hand. "I think we sort of met on the ferry."

"Rough trip." Tom shook her hand. "You do get used to it. It only took me the first ten years of my life."

Liv sincerely hoped that she wouldn't be on Agnes Island long enough to get used to it.

"Simon called me because when he arrived this morning

it looked like a trapdoor to the attic had been forced open," Tom said. "I came up to have a look around, and to see whether anyone had heard anything out of the ordinary."

Liv thought about the night before. She'd had a shower, eaten the risotto Simon had brought up and then cried herself to sleep, thinking about the misery of her situation. As a result, she had slept like the dead.

"It had a flimsy padlock, but it had been forced open," Simon said. "When I went up to check the rooms, I noticed the trapdoor was ajar in the old wing. Ambrose has no idea who it would have been and it turns out there's nothing in there but some old furniture. There were footprints, but there's so much dust you could tell nothing had been moved."

Tom grinned. His bright blue eyes lit up his freckled face. "Perhaps I should hire you as my deputy."

"I would, but navy blue's not my colour." Simon pulled a face.

"I didn't hear a thing, and it was definitely not me poking around in the attic. Would it have been one of the guests?" Liv asked.

Simon shook his head. "None of them has any reason to go into that part of the hotel. There's a ladder leading up from the wall but it would be a bit extreme to crack the lock."

"The front door isn't locked?" Tom checked.

"No need to be," Simon said.

"So anybody could have walked in during the night?" Liv had noticed most of the doors didn't get locked, except the bar. People in Aggie were pretty lax about security, leaving cars unlocked and even keys in the ignition.

"Any of the two hundred and fifty-four people present on the island," Tom said. "I'll have a look around and then I'll have a chat with some of the customers who were in the bar last night, but I can't imagine anyone has much of a motive, to be honest."

"I'd better get these clothes into the wash." Liv kicked at the bag sitting at her feet, smelling faintly of second-hand store.

"Have you heard we're having an exhibition of Laurie's work?" Simon asked Tom.

"Yeah, word gets around fast, that's fantastic news." Tom turned to Olivia. "Speaking of cultural delights, I don't suppose you've had time to do one of Glenn's night tours yet? He does a great island tour. I'd take you myself but I'm no competition."

Ambrose appeared from the kitchen door, a coffee mug and plate with a date scone balanced in one hand.

"Take who where?" he asked.

"I was wondering whether Liv had done a kiwi tour yet," Tom said. Some of the sparkle had gone out of Tom's eyes and Liv noticed Ambrose was frowning again, although that seemed to be his default expression.

"Glenn's the best person for that," Ambrose said. "I'm not sure flashing the patrol lights around is the best way to see a kiwi."

"I don't *flash* the patrol lights around, and I was just telling Liv about Moa Tours. I was going to suggest we get a group together and go out next week sometime when the weather's clear."

"I'd love that," Simon said. "I haven't been myself and I'll have a word to our esteemed guest, Julia Hemingway. She's writing a book on birds," he explained to Tom. "I'm sure she'd be keen. Maybe Malcolm would be interested too?"

Ambrose muttered something and went into the office with his lunch. He left the door open and Liv could see him hunched over a stack of papers as he sipped his coffee.

"Do you think there are any of those scones left?" Tom asked. "Perhaps Celia would like to do the tour too? I'm not sure if she has already, but it could be a fun night out. We could go after the pub quiz. I'll go and ask her."

Liv took her bag of new old clothes into the laundry, which was in a small lean-to attached to the kitchen. Celia was putting a scone on a plate for Tom and laughing at something he'd said. It must be lonely, Liv thought, being the only cop on the island, but it seemed like he'd grown up here. She wondered whether it made it easier or harder, knowing all the residents. Especially the older ones who had known him all his life. She couldn't imagine what kind of crime there would be in a place like this, and thought Simon was probably overreacting about the attic door. Chances are the padlock had rusted out, like everything else in this place. Maybe Mr Tiddles had tried to get up there to catch a mouse. It didn't explain the footprints, but could a large possum have gotten in somehow?

The thought of mice and possums made her think about the rats in the studio and after she'd switched the machine to wash, she went back out to reception to see Simon.

"Do we have a number for a pest exterminator?" she asked. "We have rats in the studio. They could be elsewhere in the hotel too."

There was a small sound from the office. "There isn't an exterminator here," Ambrose called.

Liv fought the urge to tell him pettily that she hadn't been talking to him. Did the man have super hearing?

"You'll have to call someone from the DOC office," he added.

"Will they need to come from the mainland?"

"No, there are six staff here permanently, more in summer."

"And they'll get rid of the rats?"

"They'd bloody better."

She suppressed a laugh. "Do you have a number, Simon?"

Simon flicked through the trusty Rolodex and wrote out the number. "DOC headquarters is behind the camping ground and there's not usually anyone around during the day," he said. "But if you don't get an answer, some of them usually pop in for a drink in the evening."

There was no answer at the Department of Conservation so Liv got back to cleaning out the studio. The rubber gloves her mother had sent had turned out to be handy after all. She swept out the entire area and bagged everything into large garden sacks. Once the rats were gone, she'd give the walls and floors a good wash with bleach. She peered up into the rafters, but it was too dim to see much, so it was best to leave that to the experts. By the time she'd finished for the day, her muscles were aching and her back was killing her.

"Do you have any liniment, or maybe a heat pack?" she asked Celia.

"No, have you gone and injured yourself?" There was a delicious smell of roasting lamb wafting from the kitchen. It was Sunday roast night.

Ambrose came into the kitchen with a box of vegetables that had been delivered from the store.

"No, my muscles are a bit achy, that's all. I haven't done so much physical work in years."

"You need a good soak. A long, hot shower might have to do though, seeing there's no tub."

Liv glanced at Ambrose but his face was impassive. She didn't know whether she wanted him to have heard Celia's comment or not. That it was perfectly normal to have a shower that lasted more than sixty seconds.

"I've only got a shower too, or I'd offer you a bath at my place," Celia sighed. "That's one of the few things I miss from the mainland."

Liv thought longingly of the massive egg-shaped bathtub in the apartment she'd shared with Connor. She'd kill for a soak in it right now.

She had a quick shower, which didn't really help with the aches and pains, and changed into clean clothes.

There was a lot of buzz as the locals arrived for quiz night. Most turned up early for one of Celia's roast dinners. Bridie Allen was there, registering the teams and writing the names on a whiteboard. So far they had the 'Smarty Pints' and 'Hoof Hearted'.

Simon introduced her to two of the Department of Conservation workers, still in their khaki work pants and heavy boots, sipping beer at one of the bar leaners. Sticky was originally from the United Kingdom and had been on Aggie for two years, and Erina had grown up here and left to work in Fiordland but had been lucky enough to get a job back on the island. When Liv explained the situation, Erina was keen to come and sort the rodent problem for them. They were heading out on a weed-fighting expedition the next day but

Erina said she'd be happy to set up some bait stations early in the morning.

"Do you know where the studio is, out back?" Liv asked.

"Sure. My kuia used to work at the hotel after my grandfather died, so I spent a bit of time up here." She grinned. "One of the local kids used to sell weed out behind the shed, before Laurie caught him and threatened to shoot him. So there's that too."

Rat problem sorted. Chipper was coming to start stripping the old hotel rooms the next morning. Ambrose had sorted the locksmith for the next day and Malcolm had some people coming later in the week to confer over the art gallery. It felt like some of the burden had been lifted from Liv's shoulders. It didn't really help her aching muscles though.

Chapter 12

Things were getting heated. Liv and Ambrose glared at each other across the room. Around them, people were laughing and drinking and having a great time, but *they* were at war.

"Question twenty," Celia called. "Last one for the night. What is the main ingredient in Vegemite?"

"No idea but it tastes like shite," Puff said, eliciting a laugh.

"It's full of vitamin B," Jackie said, "although I prefer Marmite myself."

Ambrose and Glenn conferred and wrote something down. Tom gave her a raised eyebrow and shrugged.

"I'm not a fan."

"I'm pretty sure it's yeast," Liv whispered, writing it down, her hand covering the paper. She was hoping she had question eleven right — and that Ambrose wouldn't know the answer. Celia had tallied up the first ten questions and Liv and Ambrose's teams were tied for the lead. Liv didn't feel like she was a competitive person usually, but she didn't want Ambrose to win.

"Okay, time's up, bring up your answers, everyone."

There was a mass shuffling of people handing in their forms and getting more drinks. Tom took up their sheet and Liv watched Ambrose as he rushed to hand his over, blocking Tom slightly.

The pub was full. Simon and Gordo had been flat out serving drinks and the kitchen had run out of hot chips. It felt like half the island was squashed into the hotel, with all the tables full. The Pansies were all in shades of purple tonight, right down to their feet. Bridie's husband was with her, a slight man with grimy fingernails and a droopy left eye. Liv recognised him from the garage. They were sitting with Chipper and another guy and had a growing collection of empties in front of them. Malcolm sat at a table with Howie and Julia, looking bored. Several children and teenagers were in the side room, playing on the old pool table.

Celia called out all the correct answers and she and Bridie started to tally up the entries.

"Thanks for buddying up with me, Tom." Liv sipped her drink.

"Not a problem," Tom said. "It's a good chance to get to know you. How are you settling in anyway? Everyone been treating you okay?"

"Well, it's been eye opening." Liv gave a small laugh. "I have to admit, I was hoping fewer people would have heard about the whole Connor thing. I've been so busy, I haven't had time to really meet everyone properly yet, but Celia and Simon have been nice."

"Didn't I read that Connor started dating that soap actress?" Tom said, then looked a bit embarrassed at having read that sort of article. "Yeah, Celia's great," he added, a little wistfully. "I was surprised when she came back after Neil died."

"Neil?"

"Her husband." Tom's voice was low. "Sorry, I thought she might have told you. He died a few years ago now. Drowned when his fishing trawler capsized."

"Poor Celia," Liv said. "I didn't know she'd been married."

"Yeah, she came to Aggie after she met Neil on the mainland, followed him here and they got married not long after. I was the one who had to tell her." He took a sip of his orange juice and looked over at the table Celia was at, his eyes soft. "I'll never forget the look on her face."

"That must be a hard part of the job," Liv said, patting his arm. When she looked up, Ambrose was scowling at her still.

"Luckily it's not something I have to do too often." He was still looking at Celia, who was laughing with Bridie, her head tilted back and dark eyes shining. "Do you get over that, do you think? Losing a spouse? Neil was a mate and a good guy, I imagine it must be hard for her to move on."

"Okay, folks, it looks like we have a tie for first," Celia called as she stood up. "But since both Ambrose and Liv's teams are disqualified, the prize goes to the third-highest score, the Pansies. Again."

"What? Why are we disqualified?" Liv asked.

"Because you own the place," Celia said.

"Well, you might have told us that at the start," Ambrose grumbled.

"And miss watching you guys battle it out?" Celia laughed. "I don't think we've ever had so many arguments over the accuracy of answers before."

"Sorry, I can't believe I got the one about the road sign wrong," Tom said, looking sheepish.

"I can," Ambrose said snidely, and Tom shot him a filthy look.

"I returned the bloody bike," Tom said, somewhat cryptically.

Gordo, she noticed, had dozed off, his head resting on the counter. Liv decided it was time for bed herself.

Things rarely go to plan. First Julia fell and hurt her ankle while out for a morning walk. She'd been startled by Erina, who had turned up to put the bait traps in the studio and check to see whether there were any signs of possums. Both shrieked, and Julia tripped over a log, hidden by the long grass. Liv, hearing the commotion, had called Jackie once the clinic was open and she came up to the hotel in the old Honda Fit that the nurses used for house calls.

"What on earth were you doing out so early?" Jackie scolded. "It would have still been dark. It's no wonder you tripped and hurt yourself."

"I thought I might catch a glimpse of a white-faced heron." Julia winced as Jackie pressed gentle fingers around her foot.

"You won't find them up here, darling, you'd need to have a look around Smugglers Bay."

"Well, yes, of course, I didn't realise it was such a long way from the hotel."

"You definitely need a car to get there. Have a talk with Glenn Moa and get him to take you on one of his island tours. There's not much Glenn doesn't know about our feathered friends."

Julia looked pale, but Jackie declared that fortunately her ankle was only twisted and would come right with a bit of elevation and rest. She wrapped it in a compression bandage and suggested she use an ice pack on it.

Next, Chipper hadn't turned up to work. When Liv called his mobile, he mumbled an apology and said he'd be there 'in a bit', however long that was.

Malcolm complained that there was mould growing on his ceiling and politely requested another room, which wasn't a problem as he and Julia were currently the only guests, but it was another thing to deal with.

When Chipper finally did turn up, Liv put him to work on the ceiling right away. She then dragged the ladder from the shed and made a start stripping wallpaper in one of the unused hotel rooms, which was where Simon found her that afternoon.

"Gosh, you're a little machine, aren't you?" He poked his head into the room. "I thought you might want a break for lunch. Oh, and the locksmith is here." Liv checked her phone. It was after two. She mentally added 'plasterer' to her do-to list and put down the trowel she'd been using to scrape the backing paper off.

The locksmith was standing with Malcolm in the restaurant. Julia sat at one of the tables, her bandaged foot propped on a seat, tapping away on her laptop. Two women Liv hadn't met were chatting with Celia as she served them their coffee, a small child in a pushchair between them.

"It's crucial we get into the storeroom so we can inspect the paintings and assess their condition, then get them cleaned up and ready for display," Malcolm said.

The locksmith nodded. "Should be easy enough."

"As I mentioned on the phone, we're going to need a replacement lock to secure them temporarily leading up to the exhibition. These are extremely valuable pieces of art."

"I've got a selection with me, but it sounds like a digital lock would be your best bet," the locksmith said. "Especially if you want secure access for multiple people and don't want to leave a key lying around."

Ambrose's head appeared around the door frame. "Ready then?"

"Let me know when you've opened Aladdin's cave," Liv said, eyeing the chocolate cake in the cabinet.

"That sounds very exciting," Julia said from her seat, and Liv went to join her. "I overheard there's going to be an art exhibition. Is it someone famous?"

"The previous owner of the hotel was a very well-known artist, but he only produced a handful of paintings each year over the last few decades," Liv explained. "Now it turns out he has an entire collection hidden in his studio. Nobody has ever seen them. I can't imagine how much they must be worth."

Julia sipped her tea. "Are there a great many paintings, do you think?"

"I hope so," Liv said. "Enough for an exhibition at least."

🐾

It turned out there were over forty paintings, and they were all of the same woman. Malcolm and Ambrose had laid them out around Laurie's office and they were luminous, even though the lighting in the room wasn't the greatest. The canvases were varying sizes, the smallest a series of three miniatures of a woman's hands cupping a delicate porcelain teacup. The others showed the model as she aged from a young woman in her twenties, her hair progressing from almost black, then streaked with grey until in her later years it was entirely silver. In an early portrait she sat, a small smile playing on her face, with her knees pulled up to her chin on the crumpled sheets of a bed. There was a set of French doors in the background, and Liv wondered whether she had posed for it in the honeymoon suite of the hotel. The largest was outdoors, the woman barefoot with the bush a dense, green contrast to the pink roses in the foreground. In the final portrait she was older, seated at a window in the soft morning light, face obscured, a silk robe falling off one shoulder. They were beautiful. The story of a life and, obviously, of a great love.

"These are incredible," Liv said softly.

"And luckily in perfect condition," Malcolm added. "I have to admit, I was a little worried."

"Who is she?" Liv felt a bit awestruck. The paintings were so vivid, she almost expected the woman to walk back into the room any minute.

"More, who *was* she?" Malcolm studied the paintings, head tilted to one side. "I'm not giving away any of Laurie's secrets."

"She looks familiar to me." Ambrose tilted his head slightly. "I think her name was Ada or Ida. She used to work in the reception, I remember her chocolate chip biscuits."

"All done." The locksmith handed a folded leaflet to Malcolm. "Here are the instructions for changing the code from the factory setting." He packed his tools away into his case.

"A bit of a mission for you, Mr Price, getting me over here and now having to put me up in the hotel for the night."

"Bloody ferry," Malcolm said. "Although at least these days it comes over three times a week. When I first started coming here — must be going on thirty years now — it was lucky if it ran once a week, and it was even more unreliable." He took a large checked handkerchief out of his jacket pocket and wiped his hands with it. "I'd have sent you on the plane but Nigel is too unwell to fly today." He huffed and took another quick look around the shed. "Too busy catching up with his lady friend, more like. Come on, I'll buy you a drink and cheese roll. Lock up here, won't you?" he said to Ambrose and Liv. "And change the bloody code to something easy to remember but difficult to guess." He headed towards the door."

"They really are something, aren't they?" Ambrose wandered amongst the paintings, pausing to look at each one. "Imagine how they'll look when they're framed."

Liv glanced over and saw that he was almost smiling. "What's in the tin?" She pointed to a battered metal tin painted with faded roses at the back of a long bench where paint tubes and clean brushes were neatly arranged.

"I didn't even notice that. Is that the tin he mentioned in the letter?" Ambrose picked up the tin and shook it gently, then tried the lid. "It's not got a lock, but the lid is jammed." He held the tin against himself and pried off the lid with some difficulty, then pulled out a bunch of letters, yellowed with age, that were tied together with kitchen string. "I guess they belonged to Laurie. Do you think we should open them?" There was a smear of dust on his T-shirt from where the tin had rested.

Liv shook her head. "Didn't he say to burn the contents? Maybe he didn't want them to be read? In any case, I didn't know him so I'd feel bad reading his letters."

"But not bad enough to take half of his hotel."

They glared at each other. The joy of the discovery and any feeling that they might have been heading for a truce had disappeared.

"Well, that's mature." Liv turned on her heels. A bitter feeling of disappointment settled over her. "I'll see you later."

She couldn't read Ambrose's expression but she hoped what she'd seen flit across his face was regret.

She walked quickly back to the hotel, leaving him to change the combination code. The man was truly insufferable.

Chapter 13

They were love letters. Out in the daylight, Ambrose had opened the top one and quickly scanned it. The sign-off at the bottom said 'Yours forever, Ida.' Underneath the tied bundle was another sheet of paper. He pulled it out carefully, noticing there was something else wedged in at the bottom of the tin. Was this what Laurie wanted to gift Malcolm?

He unfolded the paper and a lump rose in his throat. It was a treasure map, like the ones Laurie had drawn for him and Mike when they were kids. He'd painted this one to look old, with sailing ships bobbing in the ocean and a large red X on the south side of the hotel. A small cottage set away from the main street had roses carefully painted in its front garden and the town was minutely detailed. There were tiny people dotted about, a little man on the ferry and fishermen on the shore. Two young children rode bikes down the hill, legs out, hair flying. Ambrose thought perhaps one of them was him.

The map would probably be worth a fortune, he thought.

He carried the tin inside to the hotel and put it in the safe. He'd show it all to Malcolm when he got a chance.

🐾

After several hours of collating and transferring information from the hotel ledgers onto spreadsheets and trying to create some sort of system, Ambrose was sick of the poky little office. He sent Glenn a text to see what he was up to, but got no reply. Maybe he'd gone out hunting? His house was a little out of Hartwell township, but Ambrose needed to stretch his legs so he decided to go for a run to see if he was home.

As he ran, he thought about whether he ought to buy a car. He'd sold his little run-around when he came over, but it rained a lot on Aggie and he wondered if he should have paid to have it brought over on one of the freight boats. Once his place sold he'd have enough to buy a cheap vehicle off a local. Maybe he could use the other bike in the studio for now? Although it looked like it was in worse shape than the one Olivia was using.

Olivia. She hated him. He wasn't used to being disliked. And sure, it was possible he'd been a bit of a dick earlier, but what he'd said was true. She didn't know Laurie, she had no real claim on the hotel. Well, except legally. But still ... that map reinforced to Ambrose that he had meant something to Laurie once. Laurie had never met Olivia.

It was a shame he'd lost contact with Mike, but they'd gone to separate high schools — Mike to the local college and he to the boarding school his father had been to. Ambrose had held out hope that Mike might still invite him to Aggie those first Christmas holidays, but instead he remembered how long summer had felt at home, with his father always in his study or playing golf and his mother on the campaign trail, rushing in and out with an aide glued to her side.

He breathed in the sharp salty tang of the sea and the distinctive fragrance of native bush as he ran. The wind was picking up and the gulls on the beach circled like kites, cawing loudly as he followed the shoreline towards the old lighthouse, then up the gravel hill to Glenn's. It would have been a good idea to have stopped in at the butchery first, he realised as he neared Glenn's cottage. He had a shipping container up on supports next to the service station that he used to sell his homekill.

Glenn lived in a small one-bedroom cottage surrounded by bush and birds. Ambrose could hear a tūī calling from the kōwhai tree by the gate. The flax bushes were heavy with kākā and two fantails splashed about in a mosaic bird bath. The cottage itself was quiet.

Ambrose found Glenn in the small garage, safety goggles on his head and a chisel in hand. He was carving a large piece of tōtara, the beginnings of a mural taking shape across it. Glenn was a big guy, bulky like a linebacker with hands like paddles, but he had a delicate touch and his woodwork was beautiful. Ambrose watched him for a bit, leaning against the door frame and catching his breath from the uphill run.

Eventually, Glenn must have sensed his presence and he looked up, removing his ear pods with a smile.

"Hello, mate, what brings you here?"

"Needed some exercise and thought I'd see if you were around," Ambrose said. "Mind if I grab a water off you?"

Glenn grinned, standing and brushing wood chips from his jeans. "How about a beer instead?"

They sat on the back porch, looking out at the view of Smugglers Bay, the afternoon sunlight hitting the sea and the sound of birdsong surrounding them. Ambrose sighed deeply.

"Man, it's nice to be back."

"It's nice to have you back, mate." Glenn lifted his bottle to his lips. "Who'd have thought you'd end up back here, owning the hotel."

"Half owning." Ambrose realised his voice sounded a little bitter. Glenn raised an eyebrow, but said nothing. "She's going to want to sell it," Ambrose said. "The minute she has her money she'll be off, chasing after some other poor rich mug." Glenn stayed quiet. "She's not cut out for island life, without all the bells and whistles and fancy lifestyle, is she?"

"I dunno, she seems like she's not afraid of getting her hands dirty to me." Glenn shrugged. "She's been doing a lot of mahi."

"Well, she only got the place because she gatecrashed Laurie's funeral." Ambrose drained the last of his beer. "She didn't even know him."

Glenn got up to get them another drink. "Did anyone really know him though?" he called over his shoulder as he bent down to get more beers from the fridge. "I mean, he must have suspected no one would turn up to send him off, he was pretty rude to almost everyone here."

Not to him though, Ambrose thought.

"Well, I plan to buy her out," Ambrose said. "I just need to find the money."

"Your mum?" Glenn asked.

Ambrose shook his head. "I'd rather not. I'll try for a bank loan first."

Glenn gave him a long look while he popped the caps off their drinks and handed Ambrose a cold bottle. "I see she's in the running again this election. You think she'll be the next prime minister?"

"Highly likely." Ambrose slid down a bit in his seat and took a large swig. "Anyway, enough about my problems, how's your love life?"

Glenn laughed. "Mate, it's slim pickings when you're a gay man on a small island, let me tell you."

"What about Simon?" Ambrose raised an eyebrow.

"Dude, just because we're the only gays in the bloody village does not mean we're compatible," Glenn said, but he was blushing.

"What, physically you mean?" Ambrose said, to get a reaction. "You have to admit he's a good-looking guy."

Glenn laughed and threw a bottle cap at him. It bounced

off Ambrose's shoulder and landed on the railing where a kākā swooped down to inspect it. Two more followed and Glenn put a handful of seeds out for them to eat from a ready supply in the pocket of his Swanndri.

"That reminds me," Ambrose said. "Julia thought we might have owls in the studio."

Glenn's head shot up. "Barn owls? Did she see one?"

"I'm not sure, I found her out there the other morning. Do we even have barn owls in New Zealand? I thought we only had morepork?"

"They're everywhere except Antarctica," Glenn said, "but there's only been a few sightings here, maybe a dozen. And none in recent years."

"Well, I wouldn't get too excited. I'm not sure Ms Hemingway is as much of an expert as she claims." He told Glenn about their conversation. "Also, Tom suggested we all do a kiwi hunt sometime," he added, rolling his eyes. Glenn laughed loudly and Ambrose glared at him. "What?"

"Firstly, it's not a hunt, it's a sighting, and secondly, are you still pissy with Tom after all these years?"

"I'm not pissy," Ambrose said defensively. "But how he got into law enforcement is a mystery to me. He's a thief." Glenn laughed even louder, scaring the kākā, which took off in a flurry back to the trees.

"Mate, we were twelve and he borrowed your bike."

"Stole it," Ambrose insisted.

Glenn laughed again. "Potato, poh-tah-toe." He stood up

and took his phone out of his pocket to check the time. "You want a ride back to the hotel? I was planning on heading over to drop off some sausies."

Ambrose finished off his beer and stood. "Sounds good, but I'm not talking about Tom on the way."

Chapter 14

There was a loud thumping sound coming from down the hall when Ambrose woke the next morning. In his other life, he didn't drink every night. Having the bar right there was a little too convenient. Simon, it turned out, brewed beer as a hobby and he and Glenn had done some intensive sampling after closing. He wasn't used to drinking so much and his head hurt. He needed a painkiller and a shower.

There was another loud bang and Ambrose checked his watch. It was after nine o'clock. He didn't normally sleep so late. He put on his dressing gown and slippers and went to see what was happening.

Chipper was in one of the guest rooms, pulling down ceiling plaster. Olivia was helping him, dressed in a pair of too-large overalls, covered in a fine layer of white plaster dust. He left before either of them could see him, heading to the shower and feeling a little guilty. He'd get onto finding someone else to help today. Perhaps the older Banks kid would want to earn some pocket money?

The shower felt fantastic pelting down on top of his head and he lathered up his loofah, scrubbing himself vigorously. Olivia had looked different, he thought, more natural and sort of sexy in those overalls, a bit like Blake Lively in that movie ... he forced himself to stop thinking about Olivia and rinsed off, stepped out of the shower, and reached for a towel, right as the door opened.

Olivia's mouth opened wide and her eyes did a quick scan up and down Ambrose's wet, naked body, then another, slower one.

"Do you mind?" He quickly wrapped the towel around his waist, his face flaming. "A little privacy would be nice."

"Sorry." She raised her hands, palms out. "I didn't realise you were ... I needed to wash my hands, and ..." she trailed off, her eyes squinting slightly. "Besides, there was no tag on the handle, so I didn't know you were in here, did I?" She took a small step back. "Obviously I didn't or I wouldn't have come in."

Ambrose reached out and firmly pushed the door shut in front of her shocked face.

Later, after he'd forced down some breakfast and several cups of coffee, he came to the conclusion that he had probably been the one most at fault. He flicked through the numbers in the Rolodex until he found Sandra Banks. She answered on the third ring.

"Banks residence."

"Hello, Sandra, Ambrose McCafferty here." He cleared his throat, feeling a bit awkward. "From the hotel," he continued, and she laughed.

"Yes, I remember you well, Ambrose, I've been meaning to come and catch up, it's been a while."

"It has." He blushed in the dimness of the office. He and Sandra had spent the last summer he was here making out in the sand dunes and behind the library. "In any case, I heard you have kids?"

"Yes, I married Alan and we have four boys, Declan, Cooper, Adison and Benji."

"Right, yes, umm, congratulations." Ambrose cringed internally after he'd said it. "The thing is, I was wondering if they, or rather the older boy, Declan is it, ...? I wondered if he would be interested in helping Chipper out with our renovations? I heard you homeschool? He's a teenager, right?"

"Fifteen," Sandra said. "And I'm sure he'd be keen. He's pretty good in the garden too, if you need someone who can identify plants from weeds." Ambrose could hear her rustling round in her kitchen, dishes clanking in the sink. "He's gone out with his mate James but I'll check when he gets back. Actually, James might be keen too."

"The more the merrier," Ambrose told her. "Where are they at with their school work at the moment?"

"Declan mostly does his in the mornings," Sandra said. Ambrose could hear a child in the background calling out.

"He's pretty good at regulating it these days, although he's terrible at maths. Gets that from me." She laughed. "How about I come up with them both sometime? It would be nice to say hi."

"That sounds great. Whenever suits."

Ambrose leant back in his chair and stretched, feeling pleased. Outside in the foyer he could hear Malcolm talking on his phone. It reminded him of the metal box and he retrieved it from the safe, carrying it out to show Laurie's agent.

"Well, I know Laurie said to burn those," Malcolm said, indicating the letters, "but it seems a shame. They probably tell a tragic love story if what I've learnt over the years is right. And I imagine *someone* might want them. As for the map, I can see by the way you handled it that it means something to you, am I right?"

Ambrose nodded and told him about the adventures Laurie had set up for him and Mike as kids. "He hid all sorts of things, old coins, chocolate bars, even cigars once. Mike and I both threw up after we smoked them. Maybe that was his plan."

"Well, why don't you keep it then?" Malcolm said, sliding the map over to Ambrose. "Hang it in the bar or something."

"But didn't he want you to have it?"

"I rather think *this* might have been for me." Malcolm

pulled out the object from the bottom of the tin. It was a pen. Not a fancy fountain pen, but one of those souvenir-style ones from the eighties, mustard yellow with a transparent barrel containing a small boat floating on the liquid inside. It was the island's ferry, Ambrose realised.

"That daft old bugger," Malcolm said with a chuckle, but there was a hitch in his voice and he wiped at his eyes before he put the pen in his jacket pocket, patting it fondly. "He loved how much I hate that blasted ferry."

Ambrose folded the map and carefully put it back on top of the letters, closing the tin.

Malcolm cleared his throat. "Right, back to work," he said. "Let's show Lawrence Lloyd to the world."

Chapter 15

While Chipper worked in one of the guest bedrooms, Liv tackled the bathroom. The mottled green and silver wall panels would have to be replaced with something more modern but they were easy enough to pull down. It was the wallpaper in the toilet cubicle she was having trouble with. There wasn't really enough space in the small room for a ladder, so she was standing on top of the toilet seat, trying to reach into the corner to pry the paper loose. Being in the bathroom made her think of Ambrose. She really hadn't meant to walk in on him and her cheeks heated when she thought of it. If she hadn't been so surprised, she would have shut the door straight away. Or would she? Who would have known that under the bulky jumper he usually wore was a set of pecs that ...

"Shit!" Liv felt the toilet wobble and then tilt precariously beneath her. She sprang inelegantly backwards as it tipped sideways, disconnecting the drainage pipes and causing the bowl to smash through the wall to the adjacent shower cubicle. The cistern, the old-fashioned type positioned high on the wall, emptied onto Liv with a gush. Water seeped from the toilet bowl and soaked into her sneakers. Plaster and stale water mixed, making a sodden mess over the floor. She swore again. Loudly.

Chipper appeared, a piece of wallpaper stuck to his forehead. He reached down and flipped the water valve off by the bowl. "Are you okay?"

"Yeah, I'm fine." Liv rubbed her elbow which she'd bashed against the wall.

"I'm no plumber, but … you should have disconnected the water before you tried to remove the toilet."

"I would have if I'd been intending on removing the toilet."

Chipper took a step back. "Not meaning to be rude or anything, but you don't smell great."

Liv sniffed at herself. "That's not me, it's the drain," she said, but decided it was time to call it a day and clean up.

She was surprised to see Celia through the window in the door to the bar, sitting alone at one of the tables. It wasn't one of the restaurant nights and Liv thought she'd gone home hours ago. She pushed open the door and stuck her head through.

"Hello, are you waiting for someone or can I join you?" she asked.

Celia looked up. "I doubt I'll be much fun," she said, "but I'd love the company."

"What'll you have?" Gordo asked from his perch behind the counter. Liv raised her eyebrows at Celia.

"I've ordered a gin and tonic," she said.

"Then I'll have the same, please."

"In my day, ladies used to drink shandy," Gordo muttered.

"They used to drink what?" Liv asked.

"Shandy. Half beer and half lemonade. In a small glass. Meant the womenfolk could drive the men home from the pub. This hard liquor, it's not very ladylike." He put two glasses down in front of them, along with a packet of chips. "On the house. The chips, not the drinks. I'm writing the drinks up in the ledger."

Celia ripped open the packet of chips, then lifted her drink. "Cheers." She clinked her glass against Liv's.

There were no other customers this early. Celia was one of only a handful of people around Liv's age on the Island, and most of the others were married with young children. It would be nice to have a friend, she thought. It had been a while since she'd had anyone to talk to or confide in. The wives and girlfriends of the other rugby players had been mostly nice, but Liv had only had superficial relationships with them. Connor had demanded most of her time and she regretted now that she'd let her older friendships slip while they'd been together.

"What's this ledger Gordo's going to write us up in?" she asked.

"When someone gets a drink and they don't have cash, Gordo keeps a record of it in his book. They're meant to pay it off at the end of the week. I suspect some people haven't paid in months though."

"I don't have cash, but I can pay with my card."

"I'd have thought you wouldn't have to pay at all, being half owner."

"Does Ambrose know about this ledger thing?"

"Yeah, he's ordered an eftpos machine to be installed when the computer guy comes over, but I don't know how well that's going to go down. Gordo is pretty old school." She sipped her drink. "You and Ambrose really don't communicate, do you?"

"He doesn't seem to like me much," Liv said. But she had to acknowledge they'd barely touched on the subject of running the hotel. She'd been so busy with the renovations, she'd sort of left that up to Ambrose.

"I can't imagine why. You don't seem too bad to me."

"You're not too bad yourself. Especially for someone who doesn't think they're good company."

Celia gave a little sigh. "Today would have been my fifth wedding anniversary. Neil died almost four years ago. We'd been married a bit over a year."

"I'm so sorry, Celia. Tom did mention at the pub quiz that you'd lost your husband. That must have been awful."

"It was terrible," Celia said. "I stayed on Aggie for a while because I felt close to Neil here, but then I left because I thought he was the only reason I'd come here in the first place. I missed it so much though. I realised I missed the friends I'd made here too, so when this job came up, I came back." She smiled at Liv. "Simon came to rescue me and persuade me to move back to the mainland, but I don't need rescuing."

"I didn't mean to intrude tonight ..."

"No, you're not at all. We celebrated our first anniversary in the pub right before he died and I guess five years seemed like a bit of a milestone that should be acknowledged. Of course I wish the accident hadn't happened and I still miss him, but it's getting easier each year. If it had been the other way around, I'd have hated Neil to sit around moping over me, but I'm allowing myself this one night of nostalgia." She finished her drink. "Another round, please, Gordo."

Gordo brought their drinks over. Back behind the counter he poured a beer for himself. "Here's to Neil." He raised his glass towards Celia and gave her a nod. "A bloody good fisherman, but shite at pool."

After their third drink, Gordo served a group of men who had come to play darts and then disappeared into the small kitchen behind the counter to heat up some cheese rolls.

They were golden and delicious, the cheese sauce oozing onto the plate and burning their tongues.

They played a game of pool but Liv wasn't sure who won, if either of them. Celia almost fell off her stool laughing when Liv told her about the toilet incident.

"And I walked in on Ambrose in the bathroom," Liv whispered. "He was … you know …"

"What? Spanking the monkey?" Celia sloshed her drink onto the table.

"What? No!" Liv wiped the table with her sleeve. "No, he was all …" She leant in. "Naked," she whispered.

Celia snorted with laughter. "Why do you need to whisper that?"

"I don't know." Liv shrugged. "It seemed like I should. But bloody hell, Celia, Ambrose is a bit lovely to look at, isn't he?"

"Well, yes, although I haven't seen as much as you." Celia gave a leery wink.

"It's a shame he's such an arse," Liv said solemnly, then hiccupped. "Because he has a very nice one. Another round?"

Howie came in and sidled up to Bridie's husband, who was with the dart players and who reluctantly ordered him a lemonade, which Gordo, equally unwillingly, poured.

"What's the deal with Gordo and Howie?" Liv asked.

"They've had a feud as long as anyone can recall," Celia

said. "Nobody seems to remember what it was about. I'm not sure they even do."

Gordo fell asleep at the bar, head resting on his arms. Two men poured themselves a beer from the tap and wrote their orders carefully into the ledger.

Celia nudged Gordo awake. "Can we get another round?" she asked.

"I'm cutting you off," Gordo said. He addressed a man in a black beanie. "Puff, tell that so-called taxi driver to take this one home."

Celia started to protest. Liv realised she hadn't drunk so much in a long time and was starting to feel a bit woozy. "I'd better call it a night too," she said.

"Thanks for keeping me company." Celia gave her a long hug and followed Howie out to the car. "I'll see you tomorrow."

"Only if that silly old bugger drives fast enough to get you home by morning," Gordo said, picking up the empty glasses from their table.

Liv made her way over to the stairs, feeling a little wobbly. It felt like she was climbing a mountain so she started to sing 'Ain't no mountain high enough', but couldn't remember any more of the words so had to hum the rest. She must have a word to the builder — what was his name, Chippy? Clipper?

— about fixing the staircase. At the top she turned right and made her way down the hallway.

It was nice to have a friend on the island. She hoped she and Celia might even keep in touch once she'd left. After the opening of the art exhibition more people would want to come to Agnes Island, Ambrose could hopefully buy her out and she could go back to her old life. Or her new life, whatever that looked like. She fumbled open her door and struggled out of her top, dropping it onto the floor to deal with tomorrow.

Her bedside light suddenly switched on. Except her bed was on the wrong side of the room. And the lamp was orange, not green. Also, Ambrose was sitting up in the bed that was not hers, his hair all messy and cute, bare-chested and glaring.

He cleared his throat. "Can I ask what you're doing in my room?"

Chapter 16

Sandra was in the restaurant when Ambrose arrived, with two teenage boys who were arranging salt and pepper shakers into what looked like an attempt at a chessboard. He shook both their hands before going over to her. She looked exactly the same, except twenty years older, and Ambrose was struck by the same feeling he'd had when he arrived that everything had changed and yet stayed the same.

"It's nice to see you again." Sandra pulled him into a hug. "Sorry I haven't been in earlier, but I've been flat out with kids and work."

"What is it you do again?" Ambrose went behind the counter to the coffee machine. "What will you have?"

"A flat white, thanks," she said. "I make candles and home fragrance. It started out as a hobby and has sort of taken off. Alan's had to make me a little shed out the back for a workshop and office." She gave him a grin. "Perhaps I can sell you some for the hotel?"

"Hmm, maybe, although Olivia might be best to talk to about that."

Ambrose thought again about the night before, and Olivia stripping off in his room. He'd been asleep and thought he was dreaming and it annoyed him that in his half-awake state he'd found himself pleased to see her, thinking she had come in intentionally.

He made the coffees and a couple of hot chocolates for the boys and pushed Olivia from his mind.

"How does it feel to be back?" Sandra sipped her coffee. "I heard you were a teacher on the mainland? This seems like a bit of a change."

"Yes, deputy principal at Saint George." Ambrose stirred a sachet of sugar into his mug. "But the timing with this was fantastic. I was a bit burnt out and the job had become more about dealing with logistics than the actual teaching, which is where my real passion lies."

"So, what, you'll hang around here until this place sells and then go back to it?" Sandra asked.

"Well, no," Ambrose said, "I was thinking I'll try and stay." Sandra gave him a measured look.

"But what about the teaching, if it's your passion?"

Ambrose sipped his coffee and thought. Could he stay here on Aggie and simply run the hotel? Give up on his teaching career and spend his days doing check-ins and balancing the books, overseeing the kitchen and washing towels? He suddenly felt rather uncertain. He'd loved summers on the island as a child, but he'd only ever stayed over the summer, and six weeks wasn't living here full time.

"Still, you don't have to decide anything now, do you?" Sandra said. "I never thought Declan would want to stay here and homeschool. Thought he'd jump at the chance to get away from us all and head to boarding school. But he and James love the island, don't you, guys?"

"It's all right," Declan muttered.

"And you're single?" Sandra asked. "Never married?"

"I am," Ambrose said, "and no, not even close." He thought about the few relationships he'd had in the past. His last one was with another teacher at the school and it had fizzled out after about a year. She had moved to an all-girls school and it all seemed a bit too much effort to keep the relationship going once it became less convenient. The girlfriend before that had been more into his mother and her political ambitions than she was Ambrose. Having one woman in his life managing his supposed ambitions had been enough and Ambrose had decided it wasn't worth the hassle.

"Well, that's surprising," Sandra said. "You were always quite the catch when we were young."

Ambrose blushed and fiddled with his teaspoon. "Anyway, let's talk about the job." He turned to Declan and James. "Did you bring your CVs?"

Both boys looked worried until they realised he was joking, then they grinned.

"Are we getting minimum wage?" James asked. "Sick leave? Holiday pay?"

They discussed when the boys were available and settled on a reasonable rate that seemed a bargain to Ambrose, but that they seemed thrilled with.

"Only thing is we can't start until Thursday," James said. "We both have maths assignments to do."

Declan groaned theatrically.

"He's not a fan." Sandra laughed. "It's statistics."

"I'll tell you what," Ambrose offered, "why don't I come over later and give you a hand?"

"Would you?" Sandra said. "That would be fantastic. Stay for dinner. You can catch up with Alan and I'll give you some candles for Olivia."

"Sounds like a plan," Ambrose agreed, back to thinking of Olivia, standing in his room in her bra. "I'll bring some wine."

He headed out to the studio after they left, needing to talk to Malcolm about the exhibition, and was surprised to find Erina inside. She had been back several times to check the rat traps.

"Hello, again," he said. 'I thought I saw you out here yesterday. Back again so soon?"

The rat traps were all quite obviously empty, as they had

been the day before. Ambrose knew this because he'd cautiously checked them, his heart thudding as he peered inside. He hated rats, was embarrassed to admit he had a bit of a phobia really, but the traps were like a scab on a knee. He couldn't help but have a look.

"I thought …" she faltered, then looked down at her feet for a few seconds, her bottom lip caught between her teeth. "Look, I'm a terrible liar. Always have been."

Ambrose waited patiently for her to go on. In his experience, as a teacher and deputy principal, the best policy was sometimes to say nothing to draw something out of a person.

"The talk around the island is that there's a bunch of Laurie's paintings shown up and there's going to be an exhibition." She glanced at Ambrose. "I'm looking for one of those paintings. I wouldn't have taken it or anything, I just wanted to see if it was in the collection."

"A specific painting?" Ambrose asked.

"It's of my kuia, Ida. Before she died, she made me promise to find it. Now that you're going to be displaying them, I wanted to make sure you kept her one out. It's a nude and Nan was married at the time she sat for the painting."

"Ida?" Ambrose asked. He thought of the letters in the rose-painted tin.

"That's right. Nan and Laurie were friends, I suspect more at one stage, she was a bit coy about it. They fell out over the painting when Laurie had it shown in a gallery years ago, but he got it back and it hasn't been seen since. I'm really sorry about snooping around, it's not the kind of thing I'd normally do."

"I think you'd better come with me," Ambrose said.

Erina stood in the middle of the studio, turning in a slow circle as she took in the paintings. "These are amazing."

"They are, aren't they?" Ambrose agreed. "I'm sorry the painting you're looking for isn't amongst them."

"They're all of her. What a dark horse she was. It doesn't matter about the nude not being here, I only wanted to make sure it wouldn't be included. I wonder what happened to it though?"

"In a letter Laurie left his agent, he said it was under wraps." Ambrose gently touched the corner of one of the canvases. "Perhaps he painted over it?"

"That would seem the most logical thing, I guess. It looks like these were painted over many years. They were clearly a bit more than friends." Erina laughed. "Even while she was married to my grandad."

"There's something I think you should have," Ambrose said. He activated the digital code on the storeroom as they left and they headed into his office.

"You can take the tin too, if you like," Ambrose said, removing the map and handing the letters to Erina. "I'm going to get the treasure map framed and hung in the hotel." If he ended up not staying, could he take it with him? Or did it belong here on Aggie Island?

"I'd love the tin. I remember Kuia had two exactly like these when I was a kid and the big one was always filled with chocolate chippie biscuits. This must be part of that set. Would you mind if I had a look at the map?"

He carefully unfolded it and set it on the desk in front of them. Erina leant over to have a closer look.

"I thought so. This is like the ones Laurie used to make for me when I was a little girl and I'd come up to the hotel with Nan. I wish I'd kept them now." She straightened suddenly and looked at Ambrose, laughter playing at the corners of her eyes. "Oh my God! He'd send me on these treasure hunts, all over the hotel and gardens. Do you think it was while they …?"

"While he was painting her?" Ambrose grinned.

"Well, no, that would have taken a lot longer than the time it took me to find a packet of chocolate coins. I don't really want to think about what they might have been doing." She patted the tin. "Thanks for these, and if that painting does show up …?"

"You have my word, it won't be displayed."

Erina headed towards the door.

"Erina?"

She stopped and turned back to Ambrose. "Yeah?"

"Was it you who was poking around in the attic a little while ago then?"

Erina looked puzzled. "The attic? No, it wasn't me."

"Okay. Oh, and by the way, I've had your kuia's chocolate chip biscuits. They were really good. I don't suppose she gave you the recipe?"

Chapter 17

Liv had spent the next few days avoiding Ambrose and obsessively checking doors before she opened them in case she stumbled on him again and he filed a restraining order against her.

She'd seen him briefly the morning after her embarrassing mistake, hugging a petite, dark-haired woman. They were both smiling widely and Liv wondered who she was.

On the upside, she and Chipper seemed to be making some headway with the renovations and it had turned out to be a good idea to bring her suitcase of tools to the island. She hadn't planned to, but she didn't trust her mother not to soak them in bleach or put them all through the dishwasher in her absence. Now they were coming in very handy.

Liv's dad, Warren, had left when she was twelve. He'd met his new wife, Laura, through work and fallen slowly in love with her. Or at least that was the story he'd told Liv. Her half-brother Hunter was born six months later.

Her parents had never seemed overly happy together.

Her mother, with all her mental health issues, must have been hard work for her dad, who didn't really do emotions, and it wasn't until Liv was older that she realised it had all stemmed from the death of her older brother Jason when Liv was a toddler. He'd died of septicemia, which her mother had never got over, and the strain on her parents' marriage had been too much in the end.

Laura had gone on to have Tyler a few years later, and then they'd moved up north, seeing Liv every other Christmas where it felt like she was more of a visitor than a family member. Gradually, as Liv had got older, the visits had petered out to almost nothing, and she'd see her dad if he was in town on business and a couple of times when he'd brought Laura and the boys to the South Island for a holiday.

Her parents had run a small bed and breakfast when she was a child, and after Warren left, Liv had been the one to take over the day-to-day maintenance of the place that her father had once done. Practical and good at analysing and solving problems, Warren had taught Liv so many things that were coming in useful now. She could strip and hang wallpaper, do basic plumbing jobs, disregarding the toilet incident, lay carpet, even tile a shower.

The ceiling had been fixed by Chipper, but Liv had stripped, plastered and repainted two of the rooms and even managed to find a replacement toilet in the second-hand shop that was turning out to be a bit of an Aladdin's cave of treasures. On an island like Aggie it wasn't always practical to wait for an experienced tradesperson to come over from the mainland and you had to learn on the job. Plus, YouTube tutorials were currently her best friend.

Liv was in the bathroom, re-grouting the shower, when she felt someone watching her. Looking up, she was surprised to find Ambrose leaning against the door, an unreadable expression on his face.

"Where did you get the pink trowel?" he asked, and Liv felt oddly embarrassed.

"My dad." She reached into a bucket for a sponge. "He buys me tools every year for my birthday."

"Are they all pink?"

"He started it when I was twelve, so yes, mostly," she said somewhat defensively.

"I wasn't trying to be rude." Ambrose sounded apologetic. "It's cute." He cleared his throat.

"Listen, sorry about …" Liv started.

"Do you have a minute?" he asked. "Because I've hired some helpers and I wondered where you thought they would be best used."

Declan and James were similar looking, both with floppy hair that they constantly flicked off their foreheads only to have it resettle over their eyes again. Declan was slightly smaller and James had braces. Both of them were eager to help and Liv gave them the horrible job of lugging out all the old mouldy mattresses and manky carpet from the damaged rooms.

By the end of the day they had an impressive pile at the back of the hotel. It would have to stay there until she worked out how to get it down to the dock so it could be put on the freighter, which would require a vehicle.

"I could ask my dad if you could use his trailer?" Declan offered. "Can you drive a tractor? James's dad has one for his boat."

"That could work." Liv wiped her forehead with the sleeve of her Henley. "Now, who feels like biking down to get us some ice blocks from the dairy?" She was grimy with dust and cement and her nails were a wreck, but she was feeling pretty happy with the results she was finally starting to see.

"I'll go," James offered, and Liv gave him a twenty from her pocket.

"Maybe some chocolate too?" she suggested. "I think we've earned it."

🐾

They were sitting on the veranda having a break when Tom arrived. He got out of his patrol car and then let Lad out of the cab where he ran over to say hello. The boys gave him a vigorous pat.

"I popped in to see if Celia could use some beans." He reached for a box sitting on the back seat. "My garden is overrun with them."

"I haven't seen her today yet." Liv got up and tucked the stick of her popsicle back into the wrapper before tucking it into her pocket. "Do you want me to take them?" Tom handed the box over, but he seemed reluctant.

"That pile is a bit of a fire hazard." Tom nodded towards the mound of rubbish. "Not to mention they'd make a great nest for rats."

"Yeah, I'll try to get it shifted as soon as possible," Liv promised. "Erina was here recently checking the rat traps in the studio, and I don't want any migrating out here."

"I suppose I may as well get a coffee while I'm here." Tom seemed in no rush to leave. "Can I leave Lad with you boys?"

After she had dropped the beans into the kitchen, Liv retrieved her clean sheets from the laundry and went upstairs to her room where she and Ambrose met awkwardly in the hallway as he carried a pile of fresh towels to their shared bathroom. They mumbled hellos and Liv went to open her door, only to find it was already ajar. She pushed the door open and stepped inside.

"Gosh, silly me." Julia turned from where she was standing beside Liv's bed, a startled look on her face. "I totally thought this was my room. Must be all the painkillers I'm taking."

From behind her, Liv heard Ambrose make a scoffing noise. "It can happen," Liv said a little too vehemently. When she turned self-consciously to look at Ambrose, she was somewhat mollified to see his face looked as red as hers felt.

"I'll get out of your way, so sorry about the mix-up." Juia hopped past her on her borrowed crutches and Liv put the sheets down on top of the bed, noting her bedside drawer was pulled open. She was sure she hadn't left it like that. Had Julia taken something? Not that she had anything much to take. She checked the jewellery bag inside her suitcase just to be sure, but everything was there.

"I don't trust that woman." Ambrose had moved into the doorway. "Something doesn't add up with her. There's no reason for her to have wandered down here."

Liv tended to agree, but she didn't want to admit that to him. "I'm sure it was a harmless mistake," she said. "Most people don't go meandering into other people's rooms intentionally."

Ambrose's mouth twitched up a little in the corner, like he was trying not to smile. "Listen, I think maybe we should call a truce and sit down together to discuss the running of this place," he said. "Do you feel like a drink?"

There was a sudden, long bleating sound like an air-raid siren. It kept going and going like a loud car alarm. Outside, Lad began to howl.

"What the hell is that?" Liv yelped.

"Fire siren," Ambrose called back, heading down the hall, drinks forgotten.

Chapter 18

It seemed like all of Hartwell town had come out to either help put out the fire or watch the volunteers while they did it. The old fire truck was parked on the road beside the school and everyone mingled on the field, watching as Glenn, Tom and Erina hosed the old wooden supply shed next to the senior classroom.

"I hope we get a day off school tomorrow," a boy said, his eyes bright with excitement.

"Me too," his mate added. "I haven't finished my science project."

Ambrose had gone over to talk to Chipper, who was standing with a woman, her thumbnail in her mouth, looking worried. Next to her was a man in jeans and a T-shirt. Liv thought he must be freezing in the cold evening air. She had her hands tucked in her jacket rueing the lack of a scarf and hat. The man reached into his pocket for a packet of smokes, then thought better of it and put them away.

A group of kids were running around, getting closer and

closer to the fire truck, and Ambrose went over to corral them back onto the field. He was authoritative, and the kids were quick to listen to him. Liv had heard from Simon that he was a teacher, and she could see from the way he squatted down to talk to the kids that he was a good one. They seemed engaged, paying attention to what he was telling them and nodding solemnly. He stood and shook each of their hands before heading back her way.

"Greta says the fire was contained and hopefully the classrooms haven't been affected," he told her.

"Greta?"

"Chipper's wife. She's one of the teachers at the school. She was working late and saw the shed catch fire."

"Do they know what caused it?" Liv pulled up the hood on her jacket.

"Not that I've heard." Ambrose gave her a sideways look. "Come on, you're cold, let's head back to the hotel and warm up. Glenn will probably come up after they're done and give me a rundown and there's not much else to be done here."

"I could drive you up if you like," Howie offered. "I'm heading up there myself."

Ambrose gave him a smile. "Thanks, but I could do with the exercise." He put his hand on Liv's shoulder to steer her as they walked through the playground. "We'll probably beat him on foot the way he drives," he said, leaning in close. Liv laughed, but she was conscious of the weight of Ambrose's hand, warm and comforting, and the low sound of his voice right beside her ear.

"I hadn't really thought about emergency services on an island," Liv admitted as they stood at the counter to order drinks and a bowl of fries from Gordo. They'd had to wake him up, his head down on his arms at the bar, snoring loudly. "Do they have many fires here? I'm thinking that most properties are wooden, like the hotel."

"Aye, there're a few stone cottages. My grandad built one of them, but new buildings tend to be wood." Gordo slid her glass over, the wine sloshing onto a bar runner that said 'It's 5 o'clock somewhere'. "That's why most of the islanders are volunteer firefighters. It's all hands on deck when a fire starts. Usually from those bleedin' gum trees that are everywhere. They're a real hazard."

"Why plant them then?"

"They've been here since before me," Gordo said. "The whalers gifted the seedlings to the rangatira, back in the day. The roots are a blinking menace too, causing all sorts of problems with the roads."

"The old fire truck must have been here a while?" Ambrose said. "It looks like it belongs in a museum."

So did Gordo, Liv thought. "What do they do when people die here? Do they all get buried? There's no funeral home, right?"

"There's a coffin, under the police station," Gordo told her. "You get a final trip back to the mainland on the ferry, or if you're lucky, by plane. Some folks bring the ashes back to scatter."

"It's the same if you need to get to the hospital," Ambrose said. "When I was a kid, I remember one of the DOC workers being rushed to the airstrip when a machete almost went through their arm."

"Bloody hell." Liv took a slug of her wine.

"That's if they made it in time, if it wasn't Howie driving them up." Gordo noted their order in his ledger, his writing like chicken scratch. "You'd as likely bleed to death."

"I'm a flamin' better driver than you, you drongo," Howie said.

"Well, apart from that time you ran over Sandra's grandad's letterbox," Ambrose laughed.

Howie slammed down his lemonade. "That was not my fault. If Gordo hadn't egged the windscreen, I'd have been fine."

"There's never been any proof that was me," Gordo said with a smirk. "There're a lot of birds on Aggie."

"You were the one with the chicken farm," Howie huffed, and Gordo grinned.

"Mike and I thought we'd get the blame for that. And the dead rat Gordo found in his gumboot the next day," Ambrose said. "That definitely wasn't me."

"That reminds me, I'd better get rid of that pile of rubbish out the back." Liv was thinking how awful it would be to be the cause of another fire. "Declan said his dad had a trailer. It needs to get to the dock, doesn't it?"

"There's a skip on the east side of the wharf, over Barretts Bay." Gordo wiped up several spilled droplets of wine from the counter. "Dump it there and when the freighter next comes, they'll take it to the refuse station on the mainland."

Ambrose was fiddling with his glass. "I could do that," he said. "I haven't got a lot on tomorrow and, I, um, yeah, I could do that to help out, I guess."

He didn't sound overly enthusiastic but at this stage Liv would take any bit of help she could. "That would be great. Thanks," she said. "The boys or I can help you load it up. Should we take our drinks over to the window? I was hoping to talk to you about the hotel. We haven't really talked about finances or day-to-day stuff, or anything really."

Liv had helped her mother run the bed and breakfast until she'd left home, and she did want to know about running the hotel, given she was a half owner, but she also needed to make sure Ambrose realised she didn't have a lot of money to invest in the renovations, or to contribute to a working capital. She hoped that by doing as much of the work herself as she could, he'd think she was pulling her weight. But they needed to discuss a plan and, more importantly, a budget and make sure they were on the same page.

They sat at a table, both a bit awkward. It was like they were having a little truce.

"You're doing a great job with all the repairs," Ambrose told her.

"Thanks. I realised though that you must be doing all the day-to-day running. I'm sorry I haven't asked."

"Well, since we only have a handful of rooms, that's not such a big deal. A few towels and sheets. It's more that no one here seems to have moved past the eighties and the introduction of computers." He fiddled with the stem of his wine glass. "I'm getting there, but it's a process, creating a proper money trail and getting with the times."

"Is there anything you want me to do?"

He took a sip of his wine as he thought. "Are you any good with a camera? Malcolm wants me to set up some social media for the place so that we can advertise the exhibition. It's not really my thing."

Liv grinned. "It's totally my thing. Leave it to me."

Glenn, Tom, Erina and a few other islanders who were members of the Volunteer Fire Brigade came into the hotel and Gordo poured them large pints of beer. "On the house," he said, and Liv thought it was a small but well-deserved perk. The pub was filling up, rather packed, for a weekday. There were a few kids present, excited because the school would indeed be closed the next day. The boy with the unfinished science project looked particularly ecstatic.

"Let's talk a bit more tomorrow," Liv suggested to Ambrose, but he was looking over at Bridie coming in the door of the pub with Jackie and Sandra, a strange expression on his face. "You okay?" she asked, and for some reason he blushed.

"Sorry, yes. I was … is that your top?"

"My what?"

"Your pink top, the one Bridie's wearing?"

Liv took another look and laughed under her breath. Bridie was indeed wearing her rather distinctive Zambesi satin blouse, with its low-cut neckline and embroidered trim.

"She is. I took some stuff down to swap at the op shop. I guess she got first dibs."

"It looked better on you," Ambrose muttered so quietly that Liv wasn't sure he meant her to hear him. They both sat in a weird yet not uncomfortable silence until Celia and Simon came in and Liv suggested they go over and join their group.

"I was looking at the weather and Thursday night's meant to be fine." Glenn wiped beer foam from his upper lip. "Is everyone keen for a bit of an expedition? I thought we could set off around eight."

"Count me out," Malcolm said from a table nearby. "I nearly broke my bloody leg stumbling around in the dark when I tried that lark many years ago." He sniffed at his jacket, a red quilted one tonight, that he was wearing with a lemon-coloured cravat. "Do I smell of smoke? Blasted stuff, I didn't think it would waft all the way up the hill. I'm going to have to get this jacket dry-cleaned."

"I'd be keen," Celia said. "I've seen a few kiwi wandering around but never done your tour, Glenn. Liv?"

"Definitely," Liv said. "The only time I've seen a kiwi was

behind glass. It wasn't much more than a dark shadow. I'd love to see one in the wild."

"Count me in," Tom said. "I love when people have their first kiwi encounter."

Ambrose muttered something unintelligible.

"I don't have hiking boots," Simon said, "but I'd really like to do it."

"Gumboots are fine," Glenn said. "I have a few spares if any of you don't have them."

"I'll let Julia know tomorrow, I'm sure she'll be really interested," Liv said. She and Ambrose shared a look and Liv thought about Julia, poking around in her room earlier. This could be a good way of observing her. She wasn't sure what she was up to but why would she have been in Liv's room, on the opposite side of the hotel from her own, if it wasn't an honest mistake?

"Great," Glenn said. "I'll bring the van up at about quarter to, for anyone who wants a ride."

"I call shotgun," Simon said. "And dibs on the cutest gumboots."

Chapter 19

Ambrose was surprised to see Olivia sitting at the reception desk the next morning. She had an open laptop in front of her and Mr Tiddles perched on her lap, but he jumped off as Ambrose approached, tinkling as he ran into the kitchen.

"What on earth is that?" he asked. The cat was wearing a bright blue collar with a bell on it.

"Glenn suggested I get him a collar so he doesn't catch the native birds," Olivia said absently. "I don't know who set the website up for the hotel, but I'm not surprised we don't get many guests." Her hair was piled on top of her head in one of those thick hair ties and there was a pen stuck through the middle of it.

"Good idea. I'm surprised Laurie didn't have one on him actually." He nodded towards her laptop. "I thought I'd get the computer guy to have a look at our page when he comes over to overhaul the system."

"You need a web designer for that really. Lucky for you, I'm not bad at it, so I could give it a go if you'd like? I'm going to set up a Facebook page for the hotel too, as well as Instagram for Laurie's paintings."

"Rather you than me," Ambrose admitted. His phone rang and he pulled it out of his pocket. His mother. "Sorry, I have to take this," he said, but Olivia had turned her attention to whatever she was doing.

"Ambrose McCafferty," he said automatically, feeling a bit ridiculous to be so formal when it was his mum on the other end.

"Darling, Mother here. Quick call to see how you are."

"Hi, Mum, I'm good. Muddling through everything at the moment. There's a lot more to do here than I'd thought."

"But how long are you staying, darling? Will you be home for your father's birthday? I'm getting Joan to organise a wee soirée at the golf club. I'm sure he'd love to see you. At least pop back for it."

Joan was his mother's long-suffering assistant. She was a great present-buyer; she'd sent Ambrose a really good bottle of whisky last year, supposedly from his parents.

"There's too much to do here, I can't really leave at the moment." As if it was divine intervention, there was an ominous crash from upstairs where Chipper was re-gibbing the bathroom.

"Ah, yes, I heard about the Lawrence Lloyd collection. That should garner a lot of interest, I should imagine. Have you got hold of the press for the opening? Would you like me to ask Joan to talk to a few people?"

"Laurie's agent is here, I think he's covering that."

"Well, make sure he contacts the right people, won't you? It couldn't hurt Joan to let the press know that it's my son involved."

"The press don't need to know your son has anything to do with it," Ambrose said a bit crossly. "I'm not really involved in the exhibition anyway, I'm trying to sort out the running of the hotel and get it renovated."

"To sell, I gather?" He could hear the coffee maker in the background and waited until it had stopped.

"No, not to sell. I'm hoping to stay." He shot a look at Olivia but she was engrossed in something on the screen.

"Stay?" His mother laughed. Ambrose recognised it as the 'Claudette McCafferty Special', the fake campaign laugh she used when she wanted to belittle someone politely. "What about your career?"

"Mum, you know I was feeling burnt out. I'm ready for a change."

His mother laughed again. "A burnt-out teacher, how original, darling. So you plan to become a hotelier? On some little back-woods island?"

The way she said 'hotelier' made it sound like he was trading in body parts.

"It's not a back-woods island, it's a stunning place, and I think I can really make something out of the hotel. Make it a place I'm proud of and that people want to come and visit."

"Darling, that hardly compares with being deputy principal of a prestigious boys' school. Old Bill Sutton is sure to retire soon, and you'd have a good chance of being made principal."

Ambrose could hear the squeak of her chair. He pictured her sitting in her home office, overlooking the ornamental pond. She only went into the campaign office when she really had to. "Being principal is the last thing I'd want."

"My constituents are going to think you've lost your marbles."

Ambrose ran his hand through his hair and sighed. "What does what your constituents think have to do with anything?"

"It's taken me years to build my reputation, you know that. All I'm asking is that you keep your options open and don't burn all your bridges. A career isn't something you give up on when the going gets tough. I would have thought you'd have more backbone than that." There was a brief pause. "Living full time in that place is very different to spending holidays there with your little school chum."

Ambrose bit back the urge to respond to her comments. "If you came for a visit you'd find out what a special part of the country it is. Would you like me to send you an invitation to the exhibition?" he said instead.

"Oh sweetie, I hardly think so. Gosh, I'm really running behind now, but it was lovely talking to you."

"I thought not," Ambrose said, but Claudette had hung up.

While Olivia and Malcolm conversed over ideas for marketing, Ambrose decided to jog down to the Banks' house and have a word with Sandra about the trailer. He passed Declan and James as they came up the hill from the village.

"We finished our school work early today," Declan said. "I want to get a new computer chair with my wages because mine's rubbish."

"I'm saving for uni. Dad said I have to pay half the halls of residence and it'll probably take me the rest of my school life to get enough." James didn't look thrilled at the thought.

It was good that they were so enterprising and Ambrose was glad they weren't neglecting their assignments. "That's good to hear," he said, jogging a bit on the spot so he didn't lose momentum.

"Also, if I get some cool clothes, I might be able to get a girlfriend," Declan added.

James gave him a shove. "Doubt it. Anyway, I thought you liked Amber?"

Declan gave James a shove back. "No, I don't."

"I'll let you boys get on with it — oh, and wear your gardening clothes tomorrow," Ambrose said a bit pointlessly, since they were always dressed in old track pants and hoodies anyway. He waved and carried on down the hill. "I'll be back shortly. See Olivia for a list of jobs."

Olivia was on his mind on the run over. It felt like maybe they were tolerating each other better. He had to admit that he may have judged her a little too harshly at the start. Perhaps she could be reasoned with to sell her half of the hotel to him at a reasonable rate.

Far from the princess he'd expected, Olivia was proving to be a hard worker. She seemed different now, in her work clothes, with no makeup and her pink work tools. Ambrose felt bad that she seemed to be doing so much physical labour and noticed how often she smelt of liniment too. He'd tell her to feel free to take a longer shower, he thought. It wasn't as if they were at full occupancy, and it was winter. The constant rain would surely have filled the water tanks.

Hopefully the boys would help him with all the junk that needed loading on the trailer, in case there were rats, or spiders. Bloody hell, it had just occurred to him that maybe *he* was more of a princess than Olivia.

Chapter 20

Glenn handed out torches as they got out of his and Tom's vehicles. They had driven up a long gravel road, deep into the native bush with no house lights. Everyone had rugged up in beanies and jackets as instructed and they stood around in a huddle looking around at the bush surrounding them. Liv pushed the ends of her scarf into her coat and shivered. She was excited at the thought of seeing her first kiwi in the wild, but trying not to get her hopes up too much.

"Now, before we start," Glenn said, "a few things. Obviously, we're out here at night because kiwi are nocturnal. However, kiwi do not like noise. They have shit eyesight so they rely mainly on their sense of smell and their hearing. If you're noisy, we'll never find any."

"Lucky I didn't put on my Tom Ford cologne then," Simon said.

"That will only be of benefit if you can manage to shut up for five minutes," Celia said drily.

"Actually," Glenn said, "no cologne is good, so well done,

Simon." Simon preened. "Kiwi are the only birds with nostrils on the end of their beaks, and they use them to sniff around in the ground for worms, slugs, berries and seeds, since they're omnivores. They make a fair bit of noise doing it too." Glenn added, "And they freeze when they get scared, but they're not timid. They will charge at and fight a predator."

"Oh dear, I'm not sure I like the sound of that," Julia said. "Perhaps I'll wait in the car? Maybe you could call one and I can look out the window?"

"What, on the telephone?" Simon said sarcastically.

"No, like a whistle or a coo or something?" Julia suggested, looking uncertain. Liv stole a glance at Ambrose and he raised his eyebrows slightly at her in return.

"Actually, kiwi are pretty smart," Glenn said. "They can only be fooled once by a recording of their calls."

"Do they fight with their beaks?" Liv imagined they might use them a little like swords.

"No, their feet and legs," Glenn said. "They're fast too, believe it or not. They can run as fast as you or I can."

"Probably faster than me," Simon said. "Not that I'd be running away from you, big guy."

Glenn made a funny growling sound. Liv wasn't sure if he was irritated or amused. "Anyway, we have tokoeka on Aggie, or southern brown kiwi. Tokoeka in Māori means 'weka with a walking stick'. There are actually five different types of kiwi in New Zealand."

Tom had gone a little down the path while Glenn was talking and he came back to confer.

"It might be better if we split up," he suggested. "I could take Celia and Simon, say, and head off in the opposite direction. Less noise that way."

Celia scoffed and Simon gave her a shove. "I'll go with Glenn," he offered. "Julia, maybe you should go with Tom since he's walking on the flat more."

"Good idea," Glenn agreed, and they set off, Tom shining his torch on branches for Celia and Julia to avoid. Julia could be heard complaining a few times as they walked.

"Right," said Glenn quietly, "let's take a walk down the track the other way a little bit, shall we? You have torches with red lights so they're softer on the kiwi's eyes, and try to keep voices to a whisper."

They set off slowly down the track, Liv feeling conscious of how loud her breathing sounded in the silence.

"What are we actually looking for?" she whispered.

"Droppings," Glenn said. "They leave them to mark their territory. Or footprints. Kiwi have a distinctive print. Three toes up front and one in the back, which will dent deeper into the mud."

They were all silent for a bit, shining their torches on the ground.

"Kiwi are actually more like mammals than birds," Glenn said softly. "They have bone marrow, and the female has two ovaries, where other birds have one."

"When do they breed?" Ambrose asked.

"July through February for most of them and their eggs are huge in comparison to their size. About fifteen percent of their body weight, which is why the females are bigger than the males."

"Bloody hell, imagine that," Liv said under her breath.

They kept going; the rustling sound of her jacket seemed too noisy to Liv's ears. After a few minutes, there was a scuffling sound in the undergrowth, and Glenn wordlessly gave them a signal to pause. Simon reached out and took Glenn's hand, making him grin. They stood waiting quietly, their breath frosting in the cold night air.

After a few minutes, a dark brown shuffling shape emerged. Liv held her breath with excitement as it snuffled around, poking its long beak deep into the soil. It got closer and closer until it was right beside Ambrose's shoe where he stood next to her.

"Oh my God," she breathed. She could see the kiwi so clearly, right down to the little whiskers on its beak. Its feathers were almost like fur and with no tail feathers it was round and fluffy. She wanted to lean down and stroke its back. Carefully, she angled her phone and took a photo.

After a few minutes, it wandered further up the road in search of food. They stood and watched it as it probed around with its beak. There was a bird call in the trees and it lifted its head slightly, then moved towards the sound. Liv wanted to squeal with delight at how close it had been to her. She and Ambrose grinned wildly at each other.

"How cool was that," he whispered near her ear, and Liv shivered.

Then Julia shrieked.

"I don't get why she was scared," Liv said as they drove back in Glenn's car. "Why would you write a book on birds if you're terrified of them?"

"It is a bit odd," Glenn said. "And earlier, she didn't seem to know what I meant when I said that kiwi are ratites and part of the apteryx family." Everyone stayed quiet. "Apteryx means no wings in Greek," Glenn explained. "I get that most people wouldn't know that, but she's writing a book about native birds."

"Yeah, something is not as it seems with Julia," Ambrose said. "And I intend to find out what."

Liv had a quick look at her phone.

"Whoa, look how great the photo came out." She held out her phone to show Ambrose. "Awesome shot for our Instagram page." Ambrose leant over Simon, taking her hand to angle the phone towards himself more and a little thrill ran up her arm at his touch.

"I like mine better," Simon said, showing her an image of Glenn bending over to help Julia with her gumboots.

Chapter 21

The rubbish had been delivered to the skip and Ambrose decided to take something over to say thanks for the loan of the trailer. He borrowed the bike from the studio and set off down the hill to Hartwell township.

Bridie was at the counter of the store talking to Jackie when he pushed through the door, the bell tinkling. She had on another low-cut top that he suspected was also one of Olivia's, her cleavage once again hanging rather a lot lower in it.

"Hello, Ambrose, we were just discussing the fire at the school," Bridie told him. "Erina told me that Tom said it started with a cigarette."

"He said possibly," Jackie clarified. "Anyway, I'd better get going, I have to feed the Parkers' dog for them while they're away." She gave the dog biscuits on the counter a deliberate nudge.

"Right, yes, I'll ring you up," Bridie said.

It had reminded Ambrose that they needed more cat biscuits, so he wandered down the aisle and grabbed a bag, then a box of chocolates and took them to the till.

"I hear you're going great guns renovating the hotel," Bridie said as she scanned his items.

"Yes, we're getting there," Ambrose agreed.

"I was rather surprised to see Olivia on the island." Bridie leant conspiratorially across the counter. Ambrose looked purposefully above her head, avoiding any skin-to-eye contact. "All that drama with that dishy Connor Reed, the poor boy, and her breaking his heart. Aggie hardly seems like a place for a girl like that."

"Well, it seems he moved on pretty quick if those magazines are anything to go by, and I think Olivia has proven she's more than she seems." Ambrose was surprised to find himself defending her. "Anyway, I need to go next door to the post office, so ..." He looked at his watch pointedly.

"Oh, it's not open until two today. I'm doing a shift at the ferry ticketing office at ten, so the post office will be closed."

Ambrose had forgotten how many fingers Bridie had in all the pies on the island. She basically ran the town and he'd place money on the guess that she did it all largely for the gossip. It was a good reminder not to tell her too much, unless you wanted it to be known.

"Has Julia Hemingway been in town much?" he asked. "She's writing a book about birds apparently."

Bridie scoffed. "What that woman knows about birds could fit on a napkin. She tried telling me a flippin' seagull was a baby albatross last week. In any case, I happened to overhear her talking on her phone the day she arrived and she was saying something about Laurie. How he was a miserable bugger and she deserved better." She tapped the side of her nose. "I suspect she and Laurie may have been ... friends. If you know what I mean."

This seemed highly unlikely, what with Laurie being significantly older and also seemingly in love with Ida, but Ambrose stayed quiet. It was an interesting piece of information though. Julia had never given any indication that she had known Laurie, or had even heard of him. Had she researched the hotel before she came? Surely if she'd met Laurie, she would have said so. There had been a few opportunities he could think of.

He was on his way back to the hotel after dropping the chocolates off when Tom drove up beside him and indicated for him to pull over. Ambrose gave an irritated huff and got off the bike, leaning it against a gum tree while he waited for Tom to get out of the car.

"You're riding without a helmet," Tom said, pulling out his ticket book.

Ambrose stared at him, trying to work out if he was serious. "Okay?"

"That's a ticketable offence." Tom flipped open the cover of his pad.

"Oh, come on." Ambrose felt his irritation rising. "Since when does anyone here care about helmets? There're only three roads on the whole damn island."

Tom raised an eyebrow. "Nevertheless, it's been the law since 1994." He wrote something down. "And Agnes Island is still part of New Zealand, with the same jurisdiction."

"Come on, Tom, don't be a dick," Ambrose said, and Tom frowned.

"Does this bike even belong to you?" he asked.

"Well, it doesn't bloody well belong to you, does it?" Ambrose shouted.

Fifty-five dollars for not wearing a helmet seemed excessive, Ambrose thought as he pedalled up the hill to the hotel, ticket in hand. Especially from someone who had once stolen his pushbike.

Tom had beaten him there. Ambrose found him sitting with Julia having a coffee and talking about the aversion training that he did with Lad to protect the kiwi.

"Their chests are vulnerable," Tom was saying, "since they don't have breastplates or chest muscles, as I'm sure you know."

Ambrose went past scowling, wishing he could punch Tom right in the breastplate.

He dropped off the cat biscuits in the kitchen. The bowl

was still full from last night, which was odd. Olivia was in the office, doing something to the webpage.

"Did you feed Mr Tiddles today?"

'No, I assumed you had, but we need more biscuits."

"Got some," he said, as his phone rang. The caller ID told him it was Chipper but it was hard to understand what he was saying. Ambrose thought he might be crying. Either that or he was seriously intoxicated. Or both. He could only make out a few words here and there, and then the phone disconnected.

"I think Chipper said he's not coming in today. Or possibly this week."

Olivia looked up from her screen. She had very green eyes, Ambrose noticed. Quite striking.

"He left me a garbled message this morning. All I could make out was that he hated smokers and not to trust anyone. I thought he'd rung me by accident when he was half cut."

"Well, let me know if I can do anything," Ambrose said. "I'll be out in the studio sorting out some exhibition stuff."

"I'm having a break myself today," she said, stretching her arms above her head before going back to the laptop. "Everything aches. I've got the boys stripping wallpaper and I'll get going again tomorrow."

He watched her for a few seconds, engrossed in her whatever she was doing, but then worried she'd look up and notice him staring. "See you later," he said, realising he was sort of looking forward to whatever later was.

Chapter 22

Simon had headed over to the mainland the previous day and wouldn't be back until the next ferry, Chipper was still missing in action, and Olivia was working on the marketing plan with Malcolm while manning the front desk. The rain had kept away, and looked like it would for the next couple of days, so Ambrose decided he'd tackle some of the garden.

They had no guests staying at present, other than Malcolm and Julia, and none booked for the following week, which Ambrose pondered as he worked. It was slightly concerning, if he wanted to stay on the island. Would the renovations make a difference to guest numbers? He supposed it all came down to marketing, and he was relying heavily on public interest in Laurie's work, not only for the opening but as a permanent exhibit. Hopefully it would put Aggie on the map, and when visitors got here, they'd realise how much else it had to offer.

James's dad did the gardening and maintenance for the school and other community areas and grew seedlings in a greenhouse at the back of their property. When Ambrose had borrowed the tractor, he'd offered to draw up a plan for some basic landscaping for the hotel, with some riverstone gardens and hardy native plants that could tough out the harsh winters and coastal climate.

While Declan and James worked on the front, Ambrose tackled the back of the section, which they would keep fairly simple as it wasn't an area guests would use. Maybe a few shrubs and some flaxes, to encourage the birds, especially tūī, which everyone loved. He sized up the huge old gum trees and remembered Gordo had said they were a hazard. Once things were up and running, he'd love to have a wood-burning fire in the bar area and the gum trees would provide several winters' worth of fuel.

The garden fork he was using clunked against the wooden structure that he'd assumed was a garden shed and Ambrose stopped to pull away the long grass and nettle that had grown up around it. Underneath, the wood was slimy and black with mould. He used the fork to dig away at the base of the weeds and bit by bit uncovered Laurie's old hot tub gazebo, walled in on one side but open to the bush on the others. Ambrose had thought it was long gone. Forgotten, until then, that it had even existed. The pebbles that had formed a base had mostly worn their way into the dirt and the galvanised steel tub sat directly on the ground, overgrown with weeds, the tub now a cesspool of leaves and slime. A small freestanding fire heated the water but on inspection the tubing connecting it was rusty. Something moved under the surface which made him jump, but it was only a ripple caused by the breeze.

Another thing to get rid of, Ambrose thought, feeling a bit dejected. The gazebo itself was in poor condition, with some of the wall slats broken and the roof collapsed in, but the wood was reasonably solid and could probably be burnt, unless they turned it into some kind of seating area for guests. It did have a beautiful outlook and in summer it could be a nice place to sit and look out over the native bush.

There was an ugly plastic rainwater tank nearby, covered in debris, but it seemed to be full. The tank might be able to be reused. If not by the hotel then surely someone on the island would want it? They were a resourceful lot and recycling was a way of life here, a necessity because of how difficult and costly it was to get materials from the mainland.

Ambrose continued clearing the growth around the gazebo and realised the smell he had assumed was stagnant water was now getting stronger. A cluster of flies flew off as he disturbed them and he thought uneasily of the rat traps in and around the studio. Had one crawled out here and died?

There was a dark shape with matted, wet fur burrowed into the grass and he let out a very small yelp. It was way too big to be a rat, he hoped, so he used the garden fork to tentatively part the grass. It was a cat. A very dead cat, wearing a bright blue collar.

Olivia was going to be upset. It was ironic that Mr Tiddles was the only thing keeping her tied to the hotel, yet she seemed to have grown fond of the manky creature, and Mr Tiddles appeared to like her too. Even if Ambrose hadn't had his allergies to stop him getting too close, the cat gave him a wide berth.

What would Olivia do now that the condition of Mr Tiddles needing to be cared for in Laurie's will was fulfilled? Once the renovations had been done she'd have no reason to stay. He'd be scrambling to find the money to buy her out at this point, but if Ambrose was entirely honest, he wasn't sure that was the only reason he didn't want her to leave.

Putting off any further weed clearing for the day, he trudged over to the studio to get a spade to dig the grave. As he neared, something darted in front of him, a flash of tabby fur, a fluffy tail disappearing behind the building. He almost yelled again, when he realised that it was only a cat. Had Mr Tiddles come back to life? Or maybe he'd mistaken that he was dead, despite the cat's glassy eyes and stiff limbs. Ambrose crept around to the back of the shed where the cat was hiding, crouched under an old wheelbarrow. It took one look at him, gave a warning hiss and streaked back into the trees where it had come from. It was a stray. There was no blue collar or tinkle of a cat bell, but it did look uncannily like Mr Tiddles.

The studio was open and Ambrose heard Malcolm inside the storeroom, the door open and light on. He was collating the paintings to send to Auckland to be framed and stored until the gallery was ready.

"I hope you're not coming in here with mud all over your boots," Malcolm said when Ambrose looked into the room. He was neatly dressed as usual, in one of his many suits and highly polished brogues.

"No, I'm just going to grab a spade. I uncovered the old gazebo out the back ..." For some reason he was reluctant to mention Mr Tiddles. "... and I was wondering whether it would be worth restoring it, maybe turning it into a seating area for guests."

"Well, it would be a stunning view, especially at sunset with a glass of wine. Laurie would never let anyone else out there, as far as I know. It was his own little oasis. After a day of painting, he'd sit in that tub for hours, soaking away the aches and pains. I rather enjoy a bath myself, it's a pity you don't have one in the hotel." He turned back to the canvases. "I'm trying to figure out if we have the space to display all of these. For what my opinion's worth, they're all masterpieces and deserve a place."

Malcolm's builders were due to arrive soon as well as various tradies and consultants. At least there would be more guests for the hotel.

Ambrose found the spade and begrudgingly took it back to where Mr Tiddles remained as dead as he was when he left him. As he dug a grave at the edge of the bush, a plan slowly started to form.

Taking off his sweatshirt and laying it on the ground, Ambrose used the spade to nudge Mr Tiddles into the middle of it so he could drag him over to the hole. Fighting the inclination to shudder dramatically and holding his breath against the smell of decay, he leant over and unfastened the blue collar before gently folding the cat up in the sweatshirt.

"Rest in peace, Mr Tiddles," he said as he shovelled dirt on top of the bundle. Duncan's dad would hopefully have a nice hebe or some other shrub he could plant to cover the raw earth.

From where Ambrose was standing, he noticed something leaning against the water tank. When he got closer he saw it was an old bicycle. The paint had been blue but the frame was mostly covered in rust. Black grips on the handlebars had faded to grey and were cracked and perished. The bike was identical to the one Ambrose had ridden as a boy. The one Tom had stolen and not returned.

Except that he had.

Ambrose returned the spade to the shed and then poked around the hotel until he found a large, empty box that hadn't yet been put out for recycling. When Malcolm had locked up the studio and returned to the hotel, Ambrose snuck into the kitchen to get some cat biscuits. Maybe there would be some fish in the fridge. Something he could use to entice a stray cat.

Chapter 23

By the time Simon arrived back from the mainland, Liv was itching to get back into the renovations. Chipper still hadn't come back and she was beginning to think he was on a bender. She was pleased with the updated website for the hotel and was looking forward to being able to add some photos of the new rooms. The Facebook page was up and running too, and she and Malcolm had discussed getting a PR team on board for the exhibition. Malcolm had a far reach within the local and international art community, and Liv felt given the short time frame they had available, their expertise would be of more benefit than hers.

Simon breezed in and dumped his overnight bag on the floor beside him and leant against the counter.

"Do you want the good news or the gossip?"

"The good news," Liv said. "I'm not much for gossip."

Simon pouted, looking disappointed.

"Okay, give me the good news and then you can tell me the gossip, I can see you're bursting."

"Well, the shopping was a bit restricted but I still managed to find some nice decor, within your lowly budget, I might add, for the new rooms. Thank you for entrusting me with that."

"I appreciate it," Liv said drily. Simon had pestered her with ideas until it became easier to give him free rein.

"I've ordered everything to be sent on the ferry asap but I did take some photos, which I can show you later. But now for the gossip." He paused dramatically. "Chipper's wife Greta, who is, as you know, the teacher at the school, has run off with one of the fathers from her class. Apparently, they've been having a *torrid* affair for months, probably shagging on the classroom tables. Neither of their partners had a clue it was going on."

"Who's this?" Celia came in with a box of frozen fries and a paper bag full of burger buns. Liv came round from the desk to give her a hand.

"Greta's run off with Charlie Edwards," Simon said. "His daughter Evie's in her class."

Celia looked a little shocked. "Tina's husband?" she said. "Didn't she have surgery recently?"

"Yep, broke her leg at the Pansies party when she fell down the bank at the golf course. Charlie was helping out doing the 'school run'." Simon did quotation fingers with a large smirk.

"Is she the only teacher?" Liv asked. "How many kids are there at the school anyway? It only goes up to year eight, doesn't it?"

"Yep, I think there's a couple of dozen kids," Celia said. "But there's two teachers." She grimaced. "At least there were. Greta and Maron, who's also the principal. She won't be happy."

"Who won't be happy?" Glenn said as he and Ambrose came in the door, shaking off the rain. Glenn was carrying another container of pies. Ambrose, Liv noticed, had a long scratch along the side of his neck.

"What happened to your neck?" she asked, indicating the mark.

"What? Nothing," Ambrose said, weirdly red-faced. "Scratched by a tree branch," he added a few seconds later. "Outside, in the garden."

"Well, anyway, speaking of happy," Simon grinned at Glenn, who was slipping off his raincoat, "Tina Edwards is not." He was clearly loving being the one to spill the tea. "Her husband's run off with Chipper's wife. Sailed off into the sunset with him on his fishing trawler."

"Shit," Glenn said.

"Well, that explains why Chipper's been MIA," Ambrose added.

"Poor Tina," Celia said. "And Maron. Good luck to her getting someone to drop sticks and come over here for the rest of the school year at short notice."

"Chipper will have gone on a bender for sure," Glenn said. "He was drunk for four days after we lost the last rugby test match." He looked at Liv and grimaced. "Shit, sorry."

"Okay, I guess we'll need to get on without Chipper for a bit," Liv said. "But I think that banister is above my pay grade. Do we have anyone else we could use?"

"I could probably have a look at that for you." Glenn handed over the pies to Simon. "I did some venison with a bit of your stout, and some vege ones. For the restaurant to trial." He looked a bit embarrassed, but Simon looked delighted.

"Aren't you a sweetheart?" He reached up to give Glenn a pat on the cheek. Glenn cleared his throat. "Maybe *you* could see if Maron wants your help for a bit?" he said to Ambrose. "Could you fill in until they can get someone else?"

"Maybe," Ambrose said. "Only there's so much to do here."

Liv bit back the urge to say that he wasn't doing much at all. It probably wasn't true, it just seemed like it when she was doing what felt like all the heavy lifting. Besides, surely it would only be for a week, two at the most, until they could find a replacement.

"You should," she said. "The boys and I can handle it here. Besides, Malcolm's team should be here next week and I might be able to get them to help out."

"I can handle the hotel stuff," Simon said. "And hold anything for Glenn if he needs help with the banister."

Glenn coughed and went even redder.

"I might whip down shortly," Ambrose said, sneezing suddenly. He looked up at the stairs, a weird look on his face and chewed his lip.

"Good idea. Get all the inside gossip while you're there, will you?" Simon said. "I want to beat Bridie to it."

"Actually, there's something I want to do first," Ambrose said. "Olivia, have you got a minute?"

They stood outside Julia's room, arguing.

"It's an invasion of her privacy," Liv insisted. "And what if she's in there?"

"She's not, I saw her talking to Jackie in the café, so we need to be quick." He pulled out the spare room key and inserted it in the door.

"I want it noted for the record that I'm against this," Liv said, and Ambrose sighed.

"Fine, you keep watch and tell me if you hear her coming back." He opened the door and stepped in. Liv kept one eye on him as he looked around, the other on the stairwell, praying Julia wouldn't appear.

"What are you even looking for?" she hissed as Ambrose peered into the wardrobe.

"Something that will tell me why she's lying about writing a book." Ambrose peered into the metal wastepaper basket. "Ha! Like this." He was holding a crumpled piece of paper.

"Her rubbish?" Liv said dubiously.

"Take a look. She's definitely up to something."

The paper had what looked like a dozen scribbled words on it, but on closer inspection, seemed to be signatures.

Liv could make out two loopy cursive Ls. Ambrose ferret-ed around on the desk and extracted another piece of paper from under a magazine and read it.

"That little …" He passed it over to Liv.

I, Lawrence Lloyd, hereby certify that this canvas was painted by me and freely gifted to Julia Anne Newman for her to own and do with as she pleases.

Signed

There was no signature underneath the typed letter. It seemed Julia was planning to add that bit later once she had mastered Laurie's handwriting.

"Well, this is all very illegal and dodgy," Liv said. "But how on earth is she planning to get a painting?"

"Perhaps she thought they would be all over the hotel?" Ambrose thought for a bit. "She was here before we even opened the studio, wasn't she? *We* didn't even know about the art until then. There was someone snooping around in the attic too, wasn't there? I'll bet it was her."

"Shall we call Tom?" Liv asked. Ambrose scowled, then sneezed again.

"Let's show this to Malcolm first, shall we? See if he can shed any light on it."

They sat with Malcolm in the bar and waited while he read the note. Gordo came over with a bowl of mixed nuts and then started wiping down the tables nearby with a wet cloth.

"Who do you think she is?" Ambrose asked Malcolm. "She must have had some inside knowledge of the new artwork, surely?"

"She may have seen the funeral notice and taken her chances, if she knew who Laurie was," Malcolm suggested.

Malcolm looked up at the ceiling, thinking. "The name is ringing a bell. Julia Newman … Julia Newman …"

"Newman?" Ambrose said suddenly. "Mike was a Newman!"

"Well, obviously, she's been a Newman since the wedding," Gordo scoffed.

They all looked at Gordo with matching slack-jawed expressions.

"Wait, she's Mike's wife?" Ambrose said. "What the hell?"

"Ex-wife," Gordo clarified. "They divorced when he realised she was a gold-digging hussy." He gave them all an incredulous look. "Didn't you know who Julia was?" They all looked incredulously back.

"No, but clearly you did," Ambrose said.

"Well, yeah. I never forget a face." He shrugged. "She and Mike came over right before the wedding. Laurie told Mike he was making a mistake and they had a bit of a barney. Probably because she had requested a painting for their wedding gift and Laurie told her to piss off."

"So, what, now she's here thinking she can steal a piece of art because she should have received something when Laurie died, do you think?" Liv suggested. "Even though they were no longer married."

"It would seem so," Malcolm agreed. "I'd say she may have been harbouring a bit of a grudge."

"What do we do?" Ambrose asked.

Malcolm drummed his fingers on the table for a bit. "Leave it with me. I'll handle it. Everyone keep on as normal for now, and don't let her know we know." He looked at Gordo and gave a faint shake of his head. "Not a word, Gordo, okay?"

"Who am I gonna tell?" Gordo rolled his eyes and moved on to another table, seemingly unfazed.

Chapter 24

Maron was a tall, bosomy woman who looked in her early sixties, with a shock of dark blue hair that she braided to one side. She was not what Ambrose had been expecting at all when he found her in the school office on the phone.

"Well, I suppose at least it's the weekend," she said to whoever was on the other end of the line. "But Monday might be a scramble. Do your best and let me know."

After she said her goodbyes, she indicated for Ambrose to take a seat.

"Kia ora, you must be the new hotelier I've been hearing about," she said. "Maron Tahu, how can I help?"

"Actually," Ambrose said, "I came to see if I could help you."

Maron was delighted to have Ambrose at the school and after some impressively fast paperwork was sorted, she put him in charge of the senior class. It was a bit of a clamber as Greta hadn't left any indication of her lesson planning and it had been a while since Ambrose had taught in the classroom. He spent Sunday night working on plans for the rest of the week, and thought he'd include Laurie's art in the curriculum, with a visit to the gallery when it was complete, and perhaps their own exhibition, if Maron wanted him to carry on teaching that long.

Olivia had said she wouldn't need the bike so on Monday he cycled down the hill, wearing an old helmet Declan had found him, a bit nervous but excited to get back into the classroom.

Mr Tiddles the second was shut in Ambrose's room, a makeshift litter tray under the bed, with a bowl of water and cat biscuits. He didn't want to risk him running off into the bush again and hoped he'd get used to being in the hotel with a constant supply of food he didn't have to catch. It had been an unpleasant night. The cat had meowed piteously and when Ambrose finally finished his planning and went to get into bed, he realised it had peed all over his pillow.

It had taken him over an hour the night before, out in the cold evening trying to lure the tabby cat with a tin of sardines. Finally, he'd managed to grab him, but not without a serious battle. It was just as well he was in a long-sleeved shirt, since his arms were covered in scratches. The cat had not been overjoyed to be a replacement for Mr Tiddles, but Ambrose was still waiting on the bank to approve his loan and he didn't want Olivia to insist that they sell now that Laurie's cat was gone and that requirement of the will had been voided. That was the only reason, he told himself.

With any luck, the cat would be easily tamed so he could let him out, complete with his new blue collar, to replace the first Mr Tiddles after a few more days. When he'd left that morning, the cat was asleep on the end of the bed exhausted after its restless night, and he hoped he'd stay that way until after school.

Bridie was opening the store when Ambrose arrived in the village on his way to work. He leant the bike against one of the pillars.

'You're out and about early," she said. She took in his trousers and knit jumper. "Not out exercising I guess, dressed like that?"

"No, I'm relieving at the school while Maron looks for a replacement teacher." He looked at his watch. Still half an hour before assembly. "Do you have any antihistamines?"

"Wasn't that a terrible thing, Greta and Charlie Edwards? Poor Tina, I'm going to shut the shop a bit early and pop in for a cuppa. Top shelf at the back."

"Pardon?"

"The antihistamines," she explained.

"Oh, right, thanks. Must be allergic to something in the garden."

As Ambrose fastened his helmet, Tom pulled up in the police cruiser. He headed to the store and nodded at Ambrose curtly.

Ambrose cleared his throat. "Er, Tom? Could I have a word?"

"Got a crime to report?" Tom looked Ambrose up and down. "Someone stolen your trainers?"

"I owe you an apology," Ambrose said, and Tom raised an eyebrow. "While I was clearing the section up at the hotel, I found my old bike. The one you, er, borrowed. So I'm sorry I accused you of stealing it. Clearly you *did* return it."

Tom stared at him, his expression stony. Then he threw his head back and laughed. "To be fair, mate, I didn't bring it back for a couple of weeks. I'd left it behind my old man's shed and forgotten I'd even taken it, so when I realised, I put it out the back hoping you wouldn't notice I'd had it so long. I never knew you hadn't found it." He rubbed the side of his nose with his thumb and gave Ambrose a lopsided smile. "Look, you can throw away the ticket. It was a bit petty of me."

Ambrose held out a hand and Tom shook it. "I appreciate it. Come up and have a beer when you're off duty," he said. "My shout."

Tom grinned. "I'm almost never off duty, but we should have a catch-up soon."

The children seemed oblivious as to why Mrs Smith wasn't there and were buzzing with excitement to have a new teacher, aside from Evie Edwards, who was clearly miserable that her dad had left.

"My dad said she's gone to see a man about a dog," a girl called Fern said.

"I reckon she couldn't stand Jackson's smelly feet for another minute," someone added. Ambrose thought his name might be Rupert. He was glad he only had thirteen names to memorise in the next few days. Putting an end to the chatter, he told them they were going to start their maths lesson with a game. He'd try to win them over with something fun to begin with.

At the end of the day, he and Maron sat in the staffroom after the last students had left and had a chat.

"How do you feel after day one?" Maron held out her crossed fingers. Her nails were short and painted blue to match her hair.

"Honestly?" Ambrose said. "Invigorated." He'd forgotten how much he loved being in the classroom and he'd even spent half of his lunch hour kicking a ball around with some of the students. The setting of the school was idyllic, across the road from the sea, surrounded by native bush. When he'd visited with Mike as a boy, he'd often wished he could stay on the island and go to school with Glenn and Tom.

"I'm so glad." Maron sounded relieved. "The last few days have been a lot and I was worried I'd thrown you in the deep end." She shook her head. "I didn't have a clue that there was anything going on between Greta and Charlie. He was helping out with touch rugby and I feel a bit stupid that I didn't pick anything up, if I'm honest." She stirred sugar into her milky coffee. "But I'm so grateful you're here to help out. I was watching you out on the playground and you seem to have a real rapport with the tamariki already, even the ones who aren't in your class."

"They seem like a great bunch of kids," Ambrose said. "I'm here for as long as you need me."

"I'm not looking forward to finding a permanent replacement, I can tell you. Living on Aggie isn't for everyone." Maron peered at him over the top of her blue-rimmed glasses with a thoughtful expression. "I know you've only been here a day, and it's probably a bit of a step down from what you were doing at Saint George, but if you'd like to consider taking up the role for the rest of the year, I'd be delighted to have you." She reached for a Tim Tam from the open packet on the table in front of them. "Anyway, have a think about it and let me know next week, when you've had a chance to settle in a bit more."

"I will, thank you." Ambrose felt something light up inside

him at the thought. "And I wouldn't see it as a step down, by the way."

"Maybe you'd want to stay on permanently after that too?" Maron said, sounding hopeful, then laughed. "Sorry, I'm getting ahead of myself."

But Ambrose wasn't sure she was.

Chapter 25

Liv had spent the weekend painting ceilings and her arms ached fiercely, but the bedrooms now all had non-leaking ceilings and a fresh coat of paint. The upstairs halls had been painted too, and she was glad to be rid of the last of the yellowy colour. Things were looking fresher and lighter and the improvements were coming together.

She'd found herself oddly disappointed when Ambrose hadn't showed up to the pub quiz on Sunday night but only, she told herself, because she liked a good bit of friendly rivalry.

On Monday she decided to tackle the outside of the hotel. The whole thing really needed painting, but it was too big a job for her and they couldn't afford to hire anyone to do it at this stage. But she could at least sand back the front windows of the restaurant and bar, and maybe re-stain the railings and front door.

The veranda needed the mould removed first, so she gave the boys some masks and got the Wet and Forget set up for them while she headed back to the garage to get some more sanding discs for the hired sander.

It was getting warmer and she noticed the small garden boxes outside the post office were starting to sprout daffodils, yellow and cheery. Bridie waved at her from the window and she waved back, but Bridie beckoned her in.

"You've had another couple of deliveries," she told Liv. "One's quite big, looks like it might be from your mum again, I'd say." There were several large boxes stacked in the corner. "I could get Howie to deliver them up to you, if you're not in a hurry for them. Also, would you mind taking these for Ambrose, love? I forgot to give them to him this morning when he popped in." She handed Liv a paper bag with 'Sunflower seeds' written on the front. "All very dramatic, isn't it, what with Greta and Charlie, and Ambrose taking over at the school. We haven't had such a scandal since the whole Connor ..." She trailed off, going a little pink. "Not that that was anything to do with us on the island, of course."

Liv held back a sigh. Connor had never even tried to contact her before she'd fled to Agnes Island, she realised. In fact, now that she thought about it, he hadn't crossed her mind in a while.

"What is it they say?" she said with a forced smile. "Today's news is tomorrow's fish and chips paper."

She was pleased with how the renovations were going. Glenn had started on the stair banister and it was already looking better, Malcolm's team would be here in a few days and she was hoping the paint smell would be gone from the rooms she had managed to get ready for them. Celia had said they could always stay in the campground if needed, but the little cabins were really designed for summer weather and would be pretty cold at night, plus the income would be good for the hotel. Malcolm said he would sort out the bill for accommodation, drinks and meals, and Gordo had even made a new page in his ledger, using the old wooden ruler that he'd told Liv he'd had since primary school.

Her mother had sent more cleaning supplies, and for the first time ever, Liv was happy to have an impressive supply of Spray 'n' Wipe and loo cleaner.

"Come up and see the room," Simon said, when she got back up the hill. "I've staged one to see what you think."

It looked rather cute. There was a new ceiling shade and bedside lamp in pale blue, and chiffon curtains across the wardrobe in the same colour. He'd replaced the old manky curtains with plain, serviceable ones and had placed a small basket on the table filled with mini toiletries. There were two neatly folded blue towels beside this, and the bed had been made perfectly with crisp white sheets and a grey quilt to match the curtains. With the new paint and the musty smell gone, the room looked vastly improved.

"This looks fantastic, Simon," Liv told him, giving him a hug.

"We really should do yours and Ambrose's too," Simon said, and Liv shrugged.

"We may as well wait for mine, since I'm not staying," she told him, but even as she said it, she felt a bit sad. Agnes Island was definitely growing on her. It really was a beautiful place, with its incredible landscape and the peaceful tranquillity. She was getting used to going to sleep each night with the sound of the ocean outside her window, and the native bush surrounding them, full of birds. The stars here were amazing too, the sky so clear and unpolluted.

She had no idea what she would do when she left. Or how much her half of the hotel would be worth. It seemed Ambrose was set to stay on the island, and she hoped the renovations would help bring in more visitors, and encourage a bank loan — if that was how he was going to buy her out. But there was no need to think about it yet. Not while Mr Tiddles was around. Which, come to think of it …

"Have you seen the cat lately?" she asked Simon as they headed back down the stairs. "He hasn't been in to sleep on my bed for a while."

Simon shrugged, too busy watching Glenn as he sanded, his arms bulging with muscle in his tight shirt.

Liv was in the honeymoon suite when her phone dinged with a text. She was about to attempt laying down the lino squares that she had ordered and she'd watched the YouTube video three times but was feeling a little nervous.

It was a meme Sean had sent her of Connor on the rugby field, mid tackle, his pants pulled down a little too far at the back to show his tan line and the curve of his lily-white arse. 'Trying out for the Dall-ASS cowboys' was printed across the base. It made her laugh. She sent him back the picture of the kiwi and got a 'WOW' reply.

Malcolm had arranged several newspapers and a magazine exclusive to cover the grand unveiling of Laurie's work, and the meme reminded Liv that she would need to lay low while there were journalists and camera people here. The last thing she wanted was any more media attention.

A large spider was making its way across the wall to the windows as Liv laid out the tiles, making her think about Ambrose and how he was getting on at the school.

"Right, let's do this," she said out loud, to no one, peeling off the backing on the first tile.

By Friday Liv had finished sanding the window sills and the front door and they were ready for a fresh coat of paint. The veranda had come up well and the boys had scrubbed and hosed it down, but the railings had needed doing, so she was out with the sander again, feeling a bit sick of it all, despite the satisfying results.

It was Father's Day so Liv sat on the front bench with a cup of tea and rang her dad. It took him a while to answer.

"Warren Peterson," he said.

"Hi, Dad," Liv said, trying her best to sound cheery. "Happy Father's Day."

"Livvy, hello, I must not have saved your number," Warren said. Liv couldn't help thinking that summed things up quite succinctly when it came to their relationship. "How're things? Have you managed to find a job? How's your mum?"

Liv knew she had told her dad about the hotel, but he had clearly forgotten. "Mum's fine," she said. "As far as I know. I'm on Agnes Island," she reminded him, "at the hotel?"

"Right, right," her father said a bit absently. There was a lot of noise in the background. "How's that all going then?"

"I'm doing a lot of renovations. I finished flooring a bathroom this week and I'm doing quite a bit of sanding and painting ..." She trailed off, not sure what else to say. She'd been here for almost three months, she realised, and this was the first time they had spoken.

"Fantastic," Warren said. "Good to see you getting some use out of everything I taught you."

"Well, I had to google the flooring," she said, a little snarkily. "How are the boys?"

"Good, good, we're all off to the speedway shortly for Father's Day, so that will be good. It's nice to be doing something with my kids, you know."

There was a brief pause before Liv answered, but he clearly had no idea of what he'd said, or how she would take it. "Right, well, I'd better leave you to it then. Hope you have a good day."

"Thanks, love, talk soon."

Liv disconnected the call and sat looking at the ocean, a lump in her throat. Some parent-child relationships were hard, no matter your age, she thought.

"Mind if I join you?" Ambrose said, coming out the front door with the bag of sunflower seeds. "I wanted to check on Lester, but I can come back if you want to be alone?"

"No, it's fine," Liv said, taking a deep breath. "Who's Lester?"

Lester was a massive olive and brown parrot with beautiful crimson plumage under his wings. He flew down from a pōhutukawa tree, screeching loudly, and landed on the railing, eyeing them both up. Ambrose held out a palm full of seeds and Lester shuffled closer, reached out a claw and took one, then carefully nibbled on it with his big beak.

"Olivia, meet Lester," Ambrose said. "Our resident kākā."

"Oh my ... did he eat out of your hand?" Liv said, getting out her camera and taking a photo.

"Yeah, kākā are really friendly," Ambrose said. "I try not to feed him too often, and only seeds or fruit." He held out the bag of sunflower seeds. "Do you want to try?"

"He doesn't bite?" Liv said nervously, taking a small handful of seeds and coming closer to the railing.

"No, they're surprisingly gentle," Ambrose assured her. "They're actually the only parrots that use their thumbs."

Liv held out her hand towards Lester, who inched along the rail and then extended his large claw towards her. She held still as he delicately extracted a seed and sat eating it. Ambrose slowly leant over and took Liv's phone, then leant back and snapped a photo as Lester came back for another snack.

"Wow," Liv said quietly as she watched him eat. "How cool is this?"

"It's pretty cool," Ambrose said softly.

"This is exactly what I needed after a shitty conversation with my dad," she said, laughing drily. "He didn't even remember I was on Aggie. His whole focus is on my half-brothers, as usual, I think he forgets he has another child." Lester let out a screech and flew off, his wings making a loud swoosh. "Sorry, I don't know why I'm telling you this. I'm hardly a child and it's always been this way."

"Well, if it helps, my parents only have one child and I think they forget I exist too sometimes."

She picked up her mug from beside her and glanced over at Ambrose. "I don't know why I think he's not going to keep disappointing me. I should have learnt that by now."

Ambrose huffed. "In my case, it's me who keeps disappointing my mother. My father doesn't have an opinion of his own. He either does what she tells him to or keeps out of her way at the golf club. Mum doesn't care what he does, as long as we present a united family front to the public."

"I know who she is, of course," Liv said. Everyone knew Claudette McCafferty, leader of the opposition party. She didn't admit that after hearing Ambrose on the phone to his mother, she'd googled her to find out more. Claudette's policies included housing growth, education and healthcare and she wanted to implement better wages for doctors, to stop them leaving the country. There had been a family photo, taken years ago, of Claudette seated elegantly on a fawn-coloured leather armchair in their family home, her husband and a teenaged Ambrose behind her, a large golden retriever at her side.

"Everyone knows who she is, that's the problem." He looked at Liv and then back at the view. "I guess you'd know what that's like though. With ... everything that happened ... with Connor."

"Yeah, but everything for a reason, right? It brought me to Aggie, and I'm glad for that. It's probably not somewhere I would have visited otherwise. You spent a lot of time here as a kid, right?"

"Every summer, from when I was eight until I left for boarding school. I loved it. I could be myself without any expectations or preconceptions. It was stifling at home and

I always felt like I was somehow in the way." He fiddled with the bag of sunflower seeds in his hand, pouring the leftovers back in for another day.

Liv gave a small laugh. "Me too. My mother has been dealing with mental health issues since I was little but they got worse when Dad left. One of them is excessive cleaning. It always felt like I was sitting with my feet up on a sofa while she vacuumed under me, or she was following me around re-cleaning something I thought I'd done a pretty good job of cleaning in the first place."

"Ah, that explains the deliveries of cleaning supplies."

Liv drained her tea. "Speaking of, I suppose I should go and make sure everything is ready for our guests tomorrow." She tried to drum up the energy to get up and go. "Thanks for introducing me to Lester."

"My pleasure. I like birds, they seem to be the only animals I'm not allergic to."

"What about the dog?" Liv asked, then mentally kicked herself when he looked confused. "I may have seen some photos of your family on the internet," she confessed.

Ambrose chuckled. "Ah yes, Clifford." He gave Liv a small smile. "He was our neighbour's dog. Claudette thought he looked the part, so she borrowed him." He looked at his watch. "I'd better get going too." He folded the bag and put it into his pocket before heading inside.

Liv was sorry she'd brought up the dog, and why had she told him all those things about her family? It wasn't something she usually spoke about with anyone. But he'd opened up too. Was that what happened when you were stuck on an island with only a small number of people to confide in?

She'd forgotten to ask him how it was going at the school. Or if he'd seen Mr Tiddles.

Chapter 26

Chipper arrived the next morning, trudging over from his car, ladder under one arm, looking rather morose.

Liv was in her overalls, which were now splattered in paint and polyurethane, getting ready to put a final coat of stain on the front door before Malcolm's crew arrived on the ferry.

"Good morning, Chipper," Ambrose said as he zipped up his coat over the cute knitted vest he was wearing. Liv wasn't used to seeing him dressed for school, rather than in casual jeans and argyle jumpers.

Chipper moved slightly so Ambrose could pass him. "Not much good about it." He had dark circles under his eyes and patchy stubble that he scratched at as he stood at the bottom of the steps.

"I was really sorry to hear about Greta," Liv said. "If there's anything we can do ..." She trailed off. It wasn't like she was going to be making a casserole or baking cookies.

"Nah, it's all good thanks." He sighed. "Shouldn't be surprised that she left, really. She's not from the island and most people who come here don't end up staying."

Ambrose gave them a wave as he headed down the hill to the school.

"We've got guests arriving, but do you think you could work around them and give the foyer a spruce-up?" Liv asked. She'd had some lovely bluey-grey paint sent over, but the walls would probably need a good scrub down and a couple of undercoats to hide the shabby green.

After she'd left a 'Wet paint' note on a makeshift barrier in the doorway, tidied up and cleaned her brushes, Liv went into the restaurant where she'd arranged to have lunch with Celia and a couple of her friends. Kate and Becca were already there and Celia introduced them. Liv recognised Kate as a regular at the quiz nights, and they had both been into the restaurant several times, but she hadn't had a chance to meet either of them.

They both seemed nice. Kate was Hartwell's librarian and was dating Luke, a musician and part-timer at the garage. Becca, a redhead, ran a home-based childcare, but had a child-free day and was loud and chatty.

Howie arrived with Malcolm's crew off the ferry. Liv heard him tell them to avoid Gordo's toasted sandwiches at all costs, if they didn't want food poisoning, as he unloaded their luggage, and then sometime later saw his car sputtering down the road, headed back to town. Celia brought out quiche and salad.

"We've been dying to meet you, haven't we, Kate?" Becca said. "We want to hear all the gossip about Connor Reed."

"Becca!" Kate looked mortified. "You don't have to tell us." She leant over and patted Liv's hand. "It's none of our business."

"Well, at least spill the tea about Ambrose," Becca said. "Is he single?"

"I think so," Liv said, feeling awkward.

"So you two haven't ..."

"No."

"Well, there you go, Celia," Becca said. "You could ask Ambrose out and I'll see if Tom wants to double date."

Celia looked up quickly from where she was slicing the quiche. "You and Tom are dating?" she asked, frowning slightly.

"We are," Becca said, playing with her hair.

"I don't think getting ice cream once means you're going out, Becca," Kate said gently.

"Well, he might be coming for dinner next week if he can. And he told me he wants to get married and have kids — you don't say that to someone you're not a little bit interested in, do you?"

"He was picking up Tina's little one for her, and you asked. What was he going to say?" Kate looked over at Celia and smiled slightly.

"Well, in any case, Ambrose, lovely as he is, is not my type," Celia said and Becca leant over and rubbed her arm,

"And you're probably not over Neil, are you, you poor thing."

"Anyway, tell us about this exhibition," Kate said quickly. "It's all anyone is talking about."

They ate and talked and Liv thought Kate seemed lovely. When Becca, a keen hiker, began trying to convince Celia to go on a three-day tramp with her, Liv took the chance to excuse herself back to work.

Simon was behind the reception desk, chin in his hand, watching Glenn as he changed out the stairwell light bulbs, his shirt riding up to expose his stomach.

"Have you not got anything better to do?" Liv asked.

"Me?" Simon asked. "I can't think of anything. The new guests are all checked in, but I do need to go and make up Julia's room. Did you know she was leaving?"

"Julia?" Liv asked. "When is she going?"

"She paid up and Howie took her down to the ferry while you were having lunch. I told her it was a bit early, but she seemed keen to leave. Perhaps she was worried Howie wouldn't get her there in time." He looked thoughtful. "She was acting a bit cagey. When Howie was loading her luggage into the taxi, she had something bundled up in her coat and she snapped at him when he offered to carry it for her."

Liv felt slightly faint. She checked her phone and saw that the ferry was due to leave in less than twenty minutes. "Is Malcolm around?" she asked.

"He went over to the studio with the construction team. Said not to disturb him."

Liv pulled out her phone to message Ambrose, but realised she didn't have his number. Why was Julia leaving now? They hadn't had time to figure out what she was up to, or what she would do with her note and Laurie's forged signature.

🐾

The bike juddered over the potholes as Liv rode as fast as she dared down the hill, unsure what she'd do when she got there.

The wharf came into view and she realised she was too late. There was a low hoot of the horn as the ferry slowly pulled away from the dock. Liv braked to a stop, and leant her bike against the side of the ferry office. She peered around the corner, hidden from sight by the building. Julia was standing at the back of the boat, the hood of her long black puffer jacket pulled up almost obscuring her face. She had her handbag slung over one shoulder and a cardboard tube under her arm.

"Oh my God," Liv gasped. Should she find Tom so he could have Julia arrested when she arrived? What if she had it all wrong and it wasn't a rolled-up canvas in that tube? Were book manuscripts that large? What a stupid thought. Julia clearly wasn't writing a book.

The school was right across the road, but the grounds were deserted. Lunchtime was over, Ambrose would be in the classroom with the students.

"What are you doing, hiding behind there? Are you wanting something from the shop?" Bridie was crossing the road from where she'd been manning the passenger terminal. "Come on in, love, it's not locked."

Ripping out a sheet of paper from the notebook she'd bought at the store, Liv scribbled a note to Ambrose.

Urgent. Julia drama. Meet in bar ASAP after school. Will find Malcolm.

Liv

There were two classrooms and Ambrose was teaching the seniors, so she made her way to the room that didn't have colourful flowers and cheerful-looking caterpillars painted across the windows. She'd guessed right. Through the glass Liv could see Ambrose, so she crept closer to the open door.

"Okay, Carter thinks the answer is one thousand, two hundred and six, and he'd be right, which is just as well because that's what I wrote down too." The kids all laughed.

Ambrose looked up at that moment and noticed Liv lurking by the door.

She cleared her throat. "Ah, I've got a note for Mr McCafferty," she said, holding out the piece of paper. Ambrose crossed the room and took it from her. "Sorry," she whispered, "but it's a bit urgent."

She turned to leave. "Is that your girlfriend, Mr McCafferty?" one of the children called out, and Liv fled.

Malcolm stayed in the studio for the rest of the afternoon and although Liv poked her head in at one point, she could see he was busy and didn't want to disturb him. There was nothing she could do at this point, not without some proof that Julia had stolen a canvas, but she still felt stressed out and her head had started to throb.

Heading up to her room for some painkillers, she heard a loud meowing coming from down the hallway. "Puss, puss, puss," she called, and heard it again. It seemed to be coming from Ambrose's room, so she paused outside his door to listen. "Mr Tiddles?" she called. There was frantic scratching against the door so Liv tried the handle. It was unlocked, and when she opened the door, the cat shot out and ran down the stairs. "How on earth did you get in there?" Liv wondered as she shut the door, pleased to have found him.

Chapter 27

Ambrose hurried back up the hill to the hotel after work, wondering what was so urgent that Olivia had come into school.

He was loving the job. Loving getting back to teaching and interacting with the kids. He had a real mixed bag. A couple of the older ones had great potential and there were a few who needed some extra help. He'd never worked in a mixed-age class like this one, and the challenge was fantastic.

Maron was great too. They got on well and he'd found there were a few locals that came in to help with music, art and sports and it was great getting to know some more of the people on Aggie.

He couldn't think what drama there would be with Julia. Maybe Olivia had confronted her about the note and the attempts to forge Laurie's signature? Or had she found out something new?

He found Liv in the kitchen, opening up a tin of cat food. Mr Tiddles the second was sitting at her feet waiting. Ambrose held his breath as he watched her plate up the tuna and then stroke his back as he tucked in. Bloody traitorous beast, he thought, listening to it purr, before he remembered he wanted Olivia and the cat to get along. She looked up at him and smiled.

"Look who's back," she said. "I found him in your room, but he must have been away for a bit because he's a lot skinnier, isn't he?"

Ambrose could feel his palms sweating and he rubbed them on his pants.

"He looks about the same to me. I wonder how he got in though? Must have snuck through the door when I wasn't looking," he lied. "Was that what you sent the note for?"

"What? Oh, shit, no. It's Julia," Olivia said, smile gone. "She's left. And I think she stole a painting."

Behind him, someone cackled loudly. The cat took off out the back door, claws skittering on the lino and the bell on his collar tinkling. Ambrose turned to see Malcolm, rubbing his hands together.

"So she took it, did she?" he said. "Hook, line and sinker. I haven't lost my touch then."

Both he and Olivia must have looked a little baffled. Malcolm laughed again. "Let's get a drink and I'll tell you."

Olivia made them all gin and tonics and they took them to a table alongside the windows in the bar. The veranda was looking amazing, Ambrose noted. The railings were painted and the wood re-stained. Malcolm took out his phone and scrolled through until he found what he was looking for, then passed it to Olivia. She looked at it, her face still baffled, then handed it to Ambrose.

It was a photo of a painting. A landscape of the sea, taken, Ambrose thought, from the small upstairs lounge area. It had Laurie's distinctive, long sweeping strokes to depict the waves crashing along the shore, the ferry a blurry blob, moored at the dock. It had a signature on the bottom with two familiar cursive Ls.

"Is this one of Laurie's old pieces?" he asked. "Did Julia take it? I'm not following."

"She did take it, yes." Malcolm was smiling broadly.

"Why would you let her have one of his works?" Olivia asked. "I thought the idea was to stop her. Please tell me this is part of the plan."

Malcolm sat back in his chair, resting his hands on his stomach, his fingers in the pockets of his waistcoat. "Julia, I'm going to assume, is planning to sell this piece. She doesn't want to own a Lawrence Lloyd painting for any sentimental reason. She'll have her letter of ownership and I imagine she's feeling very lucky to have spotted this canvas left outside the studio door." He took a sip of his drink, still smiling. "An oversight on my part, you see."

"So, what? You've informed all the local art dealers?" Ambrose asked, feeling a little irritated. "What if she takes it further afield?"

Malcolm chuckled again. "It won't matter who she takes it to, Julia Newman is about to find out that a 'Malcolm Price' is worth a considerable amount less than an original Lawrence Lloyd." He raised his glass in cheers.

"Wait." Olivia took another look at the photo, zooming in. "*You* painted this?"

"I was a bit of a dab hand at painting, back in the day," Malcolm told her. "Even if I do say so myself. Laurie and I met in art school, in fact."

Ambrose laughed. "You cunning old bugger," he said, raising his glass.

Olivia picked hers up, a big grin on her face. She was quite beautiful, Ambrose thought.

"To Malcolm Price, master forger," she said, and they all clinked glasses. "You don't want to paint a few landscapes to replace the shitty art in the hotel, do you?"

Ambrose changed into jeans and a sweater and quietly removed the litter box and dishes from his room, now that the cat was out of the bag, so to speak, before heading out to the back of the hotel.

He'd not had much time to clear the backyard since he was busy all day at the school, but he'd organised the boys to cut back some more of the brush for him on the weekend and he was slowly tackling things each evening, clearing a little bit here and there. He'd decided he wanted to try to clean up the old hot tub and Sandra had given him some pink stuff that worked a treat. Glenn had said he might have time to help him fix up the gazebo too, if Ambrose gave him a hand with his pies. Hopefully that meant rolling pastry and not butchering deer.

Once the back garden was all done, he planned to surprise Olivia with it.

The bar was full that night, with locals and Malcolm's construction team filling the tables. Celia and Simon had run out of so much food that several of the customers had resorted to trying Glenn's vegetarian pies.

"This is actually delicious," Jackie said. "What made you think to mix pine nuts and cauliflower? Well done, Glenn."

"I felt a bit inspired," Glenn mumbled, going pink.

"Horny, more like," Ambrose said under his breath, and Olivia laughed. He liked her laugh, liked seeing her happy. He was looking forward to seeing her face when he surprised her with the hot tub. He didn't really think of himself as a romantic guy, but maybe he'd just never met the right woman?

One of Malcolm's workers was headed up to the counter to get a round of drinks and Ambrose watched with amusement as Howie intercepted him to ask for an orange juice.

"Do you know why Gordo and Howie are at war?" he asked Malcolm. Malcolm frowned, trying to recall.

"Something to do with Howie running someone over, I believe," Malcolm said. "Gordo's mother maybe, or his aunt?"

"Shit, really?" Ambrose said, "I didn't realise it was something serious. Was she all right?"

Malcolm laughed. "Of course she was. I think he just squashed the toe on her boot, I mean, have you seen how slowly Howie drives?"

Chapter 28

Now that Julia had gone, Liv was able to revamp her empty room and she moved Malcolm to one of the newly renovated rooms so they could do his too. Aside from a new shower unit for the honeymoon suite that was due to arrive, these were the last two rooms on that side of the hotel to be done. Ambrose and Liv's rooms could wait. Liv wondered whether Ambrose might even want to convert that wing into owners' quarters once she'd left.

The thought of leaving Agnes Island made her feel a bit downcast. She would miss the people, and the sheer beauty of the place had grown on her. The last couple of mornings she'd taken her coffee outside and fed Lester a handful of seeds, expecting to see Ambrose there, but he hadn't been. She'd miss Lester too.

Liv wasn't sure if Aggie had gotten under her skin or if she was apprehensive about what lay ahead when she got back. She didn't even know where she'd go back to. Lately she'd been toying with the idea of starting a PR company of her own, but Renfield Reed was a man to hold a grudge, and she knew he would make things as difficult as he could for her. After all, she'd jilted his precious son and would feel like Liv had made their family a laughing stock. Once Ambrose had bought her half of the hotel, she'd have a bit of money to put into something — but what? It was all too much to think about right now.

The exhibition space was looking incredible. Malcolm had a real vision for it, which Liv had to admit she hadn't been able to see earlier. After she'd given Lester his seeds, she took a coffee over to Malcolm to check progress from the day before. She bumped into Ambrose coming around from the back of the hotel.

"Shit," she said, spilling half of Malcolm's coffee down the front of her overalls.

"God, sorry, I wasn't expecting you to be there. I hope that wasn't hot?" He dabbed at her front with a rag he was carrying. It smelt like wood stain and didn't really help the state of her overalls at all. Ambrose turned a bit pink and stopped dabbing.

"Actually, I wanted to talk to you about pulling up the carpet runner on the stairs, and in the upstairs hallway," Liv said.

"Can it wait until tonight? I'm running a bit behind and I need to have a shower before school."

"I guess so, but I was really hoping to make a start on it today. Glenn was telling me that the floorboards are tōtara, so I thought we could sand them ..."

"Sure, whatever you think's best."

"It would be nice to have your opinion on something for a change." She was a bit sick of making most of the decisions herself and Ambrose had seemed even more absent over the last week. He never seemed to be around after school when she needed to check on something with him.

"My opinion is that you're doing a great job," he said, sliding past her and hurrying off with a wave.

With Simon and Celia running the hotel and restaurant and Liv doing the renovations, she had started to wonder what Ambrose was doing to contribute. Glenn had carved a stunning banister for the hotel, with a kōwhai flower and koru pattern running under the handrail, and Ambrose had helped him to install that, but hadn't been around much to help with anything else. Liv felt guilty for feeling resentful. He was working full time at the school, and she knew it was because he wanted to buy her share of the hotel and he'd paid for most of the materials they'd needed, but it was a bit of a hard slog on her own, even with Chipper and the boys helping.

Malcolm had generously lent his crew, and the electrician had installed a new chandelier in the reception area. Puff had been a plumber back in the day and had come out of retirement to help with the bathrooms and kitchenette in the gallery, and would install the new shower unit when it arrived. But Liv would still have liked a bit more input from the other half-owner.

Liv handed Malcolm his coffee. "Sorry, half a cup today, I'm wearing the rest of it."

She looked around the studio space. The concrete floor was sanded and polished, the beams were freshly stained and looked fantastic against the granite walls of the shed. Framework had been set up to display the art. Electrical cords snaked across the floor as two electricians worked on the lighting. Toilets now took up the corner next to the office, which had a new window looking out into the gallery. "This is looking amazing, Malcolm, you must be pleased."

"Very pleased indeed. Everything's going to plan so far, touch wood," Malcolm said, as he reached over and tapped on a wooden frame with his hand. "Laurie would have hated all this fuss."

"I wonder what Ida would have thought?"

"Ida always seemed a rather private woman. She worked here in the hotel for years, but I never got to know her. I was aware she was the subject of Laurie's nude, the one that first brought him to the attention of the art world, but I didn't know they'd been carrying on all these years. She seemed very fond of him though. Or at least, she was one of the few people who managed to put up with him." He lapsed into silence and Liv patted his shoulder.

"I'd better get back to it," she said, "but I'd be willing to bet Laurie would secretly love all this fuss."

"You're probably right." Malcolm smiled, patting the pocket of his jacket where he kept Laurie's pen. "And he'd laugh his head off that I was stuck on this blasted island this long."

Liv took a breath and braced herself for another day of work. Simon was clearing out the reception area so that Glenn could restore the lovely kauri counter to its original state. The carved pattern on the front of the desk was encrusted with years of dirt and grime, but had been the inspiration for the handrail he'd carved. The railing gleamed, honey coloured in the morning light, and Liv ran her hand over the warm wood.

"I can't get over how incredible this looks," she said. "What a transformation it makes to the front foyer."

"And doesn't it smell delicious? Glenn's very skilled with his hands, isn't he?" Simon smirked. "By the way, I ordered some new office supplies and when I picked them up from Bridie, this box had arrived from Hardware Haven. Did you order some outdoor lamps?"

Liv lifted one edge and looked inside. "Nope, not me, you'll have to ask Ambrose." Typical, she thought. He's never around to discuss any ideas she has but now he's gone and bought decor for the front garden without checking with her.

She headed up the stairs to have a go at ripping up the carpet runner, feeling fuelled with irritation. It came away surprisingly easily, ripping off in one clean piece, the nails holding it down popping off with a satisfying sound. Dust flew up with it, decades of it, filling the air with a musty haze and Liv coughed, wishing she'd put on a mask. Her mother would be horrified, conjuring up tuberculosis or some other nasty disease.

Mr Tiddles wandered over to sit on the end of the carpet, circling around and getting comfortable as Liv tried to roll it up, making her laugh.

"Come on, get off," she said, and he opened one eye, looked at her with mild irritation, and closed it again.

Had he always had green eyes? Liv wondered. She could have sworn they were amber.

Chapter 29

By Thursday afternoon the studio was close to being done. The air-conditioning specialist was arriving on Monday, if the weather held, to install some state-of-the-art temperature-monitoring gadgets and humidifiers as well as air-filtration systems. Ambrose was amazed to see how quickly the crew had made the old studio into a beautiful heritage-style building.

The boys had turned out to be hard workers, and they'd pitched in wherever necessary. Declan had been the one to notice the old golf cart, now parked outside the studio under a tarp.

"Man, this is cool," he said. "Does it go?" He jimmied open the back panel to look at the engine.

"Olivia didn't seem to think so," Ambrose said. "It's probably been sitting around for years, unused."

Declan had already unclipped the battery and was poking around in the engine. "It definitely needs a new battery, but it's in pretty good nick. Maybe a service, brake lines, wheel bearings for sure."

"You sound like you know a bit about engines?" Ambrose said, and Declan nodded vigorously.

"He worked at the garage last summer," James said.

"I want to be a mechanic. Gavin says he'll give me a job in his workshop when I leave school. Can we have a go at fixing this?" Declan wiped his hands on his track pants.

Ambrose thought about it for a bit. It would be good to have the cart for guest pick-ups, and as a run-around in bad weather. "What sort of money are we talking about?"

"I reckon the new battery would be the biggest expense. They're not cheap. But I can see if Gavin has anything in the workshop. He's got part of an old cart similar to this down there that I might be able to use for parts."

"Okay, go for it," Ambrose agreed. "But don't let Tom see you driving it if you do get it up and running, and stay off the roads."

Ambrose was still loving the job. He knew all the kids' names now, and most of the parents, and been warmly welcomed by all of them.

He and Maron had settled nicely into a routine with breaks, playground duties and staff meetings and it was all a seemingly laid-back but well-run machine.

Maron was a fabulous principal with no plans to leave

herself, since she was married to the other health nurse who worked with Jackie and they loved island life. She already had an application with the Ministry for a third, part-time, teacher so she could reduce her classroom hours and had told Ambrose he could switch that up if he was interested in full- or part-time work in the new year. It would certainly take the financial strain off while he got the hotel up and running a little better.

The bank had approved his loan, dependent on the evaluation, so he suspected he could almost afford to buy Olivia out once the hotel was ready, but Mr Tiddles the second was keeping that from happening and he was glad. He was used to having Olivia around, and found himself looking forward to seeing her in the evenings.

The back section had come along nicely. He'd managed to get the foliage trimmed back, the lawn mowed and the edges cut along the stone pathway out to the gazebo area. He'd stood around passing Glenn nails and holding pieces of wood when told to, and they had managed to fix some decking around the tub and retain some of the gazebo for stringing up fairy lights. His solar lights had arrived and he had placed those along the pathway and on the deck. It just needed a test run, and he was rather looking forward to it after he met Tom for a drink in the bar.

Tom was out of uniform for a change but still officially on duty, so while Ambrose poured himself a beer, Tom had a lemonade. They sat at one of the high tables waiting for Celia to come and take their food order.

"So, how long have you been in love with Celia?" Ambrose asked and then grinned as Tom almost choked on his drink.

"What? How ...? Shit. Is it that obvious?" Tom gave Celia another lingering look, full of longing as she delivered a bowl of chips to a customer and then turned, skirt swirling around her legs to take an order from some of the workmen.

"Well, it is to me," Ambrose grinned.

"Bloody hell, I'm pathetic." Tom slumped down a little in his seat.

"Have you asked her out?" Ambrose asked.

Tom shook his head. "Mate, I can still remember the day I met her. She came over with Neil on the ferry and when he introduced us, I felt like I'd been punched in the gut. But she was in love with Neil, and he was a good mate, so I ignored it." He rubbed his thumb across the scruff on his chin. "Then after he died, and she left Aggie, I realised that feeling hadn't gone." He looked over at Celia again, his eyes soft. "It felt like a second chance when she came back, but ..." He looked at Ambrose and shrugged.

"So ask her out."

"What if she says no?" Tom fiddled with his glass. "I'm scared she still sees me as a mate. What if she's not over Neil? She hasn't dated anyone else while she's been back."

"What if she says yes? Only one way to find out."

"True, but to be fair, mate, I'm not sure you're exactly the best person for romantic advice, are you?"

"What does that mean?"

"Glenn tells me you're an eternal bachelor."

Ambrose thought about his past relationships and how he had never really cared enough to make them work. "I suppose I just haven't met the right one yet." He looked over at Olivia, who was sitting at the bar with Simon, and wondered if he should take his own advice.

The bath was full of water from the tank. He'd had to let it run over until the slightly murky-looking water had run clear and didn't smell. Puff had replaced the pipework for him and he'd used some of the damaged gazebo wood to light the fire.

Ambrose dipped one hand into the bath, testing to see if it was ready. It was warm, but not overly hot, so he hung up his towel on the peg nailed to the support post and stripped off, getting into the water anyway, assuming it would heat up. The water sloshed over the edge as he sank down, and he sighed, lying back and closing his eyes.

It was serenely quiet, just a distant morepork calling and the rustle of trees, and Ambrose dozed off a little, his muscles relaxing. Olivia would love this, he thought. There might even be room for two … except it was suddenly rather hot. The metal basin was hot to touch on his arms as he sat up and then there was a painful burning feeling on his arse and thighs and he had to leap up, his feet scalding on the base as he clambered out.

"You've got far too much wood in that thing," Gordo said, sauntering past. "You only need a handful." Ambrose let out a yelp, spinning round and knocking his towel off the hook, where it dropped straight into one end of the tub and sank soggily to the bottom.

"Bloody hell, Gordo," Ambrose said, grabbing at his own handful. "Give a guy a bit of warning!"

"Leave the water in, will ya?" Gordo said. "I might have a soak after you."

Chapter 30

Liv was exhausted. She'd spent all day cleaning walls, polishing railings and washing windows. Everything ached. Hartwell Hotel was clean enough for her mother to eat off and Liv was dying for a burger and a beer.

The bar was full. Erina and several DOC workers were playing pool and Jackie and the Pansies were having a game night, set up on the larger table by the back wall. A couple of families were finishing up meals and there was a group of five guys who had come in off one of the boats. Simon told her they were there for a week-long stag do.

One of the guys was at the bar, his generous belly pressed up against the wood, and when he saw Liv his eyebrows raised in recognition.

"Bloody hell, if it isn't Reed's devil woman," he said loudly. "Look at this, will you, guys, the Connor Curse, hiding away at the bottom of the world."

"Now hang on," Gordo said, pulling back on the beer handle, "there's no need for any of that."

"Trev, mate, leave it, will you," one of his friends called out.

Liv could feel her face flaming. Her stomach knotted up. She'd been here on Aggie for so long that the whole Connor Reed incident felt like it had passed, but she'd forgotten that the world off the island still thought they had reason to hate her. The All Blacks were still losing, after all, and she was the scapegoat.

"Bloody hell, look at you, you've stepped down in the world, haven't you," Trev continued, scanning her up and down. "How the mighty have fallen."

"I think that might be a little ironic coming from you," Simon said, standing on his tiptoes at the bar and puffing up slightly. "You could pass for Ozzy Osbourne's fat brother."

"You stay out of it, you little sissy," Trev said, and Glenn and Ambrose rose from their chairs.

"Gordo, call Tom, will you," Ambrose said, his hand on Glenn's shoulder, holding him back, "while I ask this guy politely to leave."

"And what is 'Tom' going to do?" another of the guys asked, coming up beside Trev.

"Arrest you?" Ambrose said casually. "Since he's a cop."

Trev scoffed. "Arrest us for what?"

"For trespassing, most likely," Ambrose said, "since the woman you're being such an arse to *owns* the hotel."

"Now hang on, mate," the other guy said, taking off his cap and turning it around to face the front. "Let's not be hasty. We don't want any trouble, do we, Trev?" He put out a hand for Ambrose to shake, which he ignored. "We'll get out of here, right, Trev? Take our beer to go, yeah?"

Gordo gave Ambrose a questioning look. Ambrose looked at Liv. "Your call."

She wanted to tell Gordo not to serve them, but they were customers, and the hotel needed the money since it also operated as a bottle shop and the markup was good.

"Fine," she said. "But apologise to Simon first."

Trev looked a bit blank. "Who?"

"That would be me," Simon said with a grin. "The sissy."

No longer in the mood to eat, Liv went back up the stairs to her room. She lay on her bed, staring at the ceiling, and willed herself not to cry. She would have to toughen up. When she did leave here, there would be plenty of people who still recognised her. Still blamed her and hated her, wherever she went.

There was a knock at her door. Ambrose was standing there, looking worried.

"Thought you might be hungry," he said, handing over a plate with sausages and mash and a glass of juice.

"Thanks, Ambrose," Liv said, "and thanks for having my back downstairs."

He blushed slightly. "Did you pack a bikini?" he asked, seemingly at random.

"Pardon?"

"A bikini, do you have one? Or something to swim in?"

Liv wondered if Trev had punched him in the head. "Yes. Why? Because last time I looked there was no indoor pool. Were you planning on taking a night trip to the beach? Because I'll pass, thanks."

Ambrose grinned. "It's a surprise," he said. "Get changed and meet me downstairs in the foyer in half an hour, okay?"

There was soft music coming from the back of the building as Liv followed Ambrose, her dressing gown wrapped tightly around her, as he led her down the now tidy path, illuminated by the solar lights he'd purchased. They rounded the side of a wooden gazebo and she stopped short. Fairy lights twinkled in the trees and standing against the backdrop of the native bush was a steel bathtub, steam rising from the water where flower petals were floating.

It felt like she had stepped into a fever dream.

"I've been fixing it up for you," Ambrose said quietly. "I thought it might be nice to have a soak after all the hard work you've been doing."

"This is amazing," Liv said. "I can't believe it."

"There's a towel there," Ambrose told her. "And I think I've got the temperature right. I put some bath salts in too, so don't put your head under." He seemed so pleased with himself, and Liv had to stop herself from crying at how lovely the whole thing was. She took off her dressing gown and looked around, wondering where to put it.

"Here, let me," Ambrose said, taking it from her. "I'll hang it up for you."

The water was hot to her cold feet as she climbed in, but perfect as her body sank lower. It smelt of lavender and Liv let out a contented sigh. "There's a glass of wine on the little ledge next to you."

Liv looked over and saw the flute, next to an unlit candle.

"Oops, that's for the mozzies," Ambrose said. "I'll just get that going ..." He leant over her to light the wick, the smell of his aftershave washing over her, woody and masculine. As he pulled back, their eyes met. His were lovely, Liv thought, with such long thick eyelashes. For a second, Liv wondered if he was going to kiss her and she realised with a jolt that she hoped he would.

"Ambrose ..." she started. She had the sudden urge to ask him to get into the tub with her.

"Right, well ... I'll leave you to it," Ambrose said, cutting her off. "Enjoy."

Liv watched him as he turned to head back down the path, a weird tightness in her chest.

"Thank you," she called to his retreating back.

Chapter 31

Liv took the day off on Saturday and was sitting outside with Celia having a coffee when the police cruiser pulled into the hotel. It was still chilly, so they were bundled up in puffer jackets, but the air felt fresh and the sky was clear, the spring sun warm against her face.

"I can't believe you haven't been around the island yet." Celia broke the giant-sized Anzac biscuit in two and offered half to Liv.

"I know, I'm going to take one of Glenn's tours when he starts up again, if I'm still here, but with the renos, it's been pretty flat out."

"I could take you for a drive sometime. Tourist season won't really ramp up for another few weeks, but you've got to see Taylor's Rise. It's the southernmost point on the island. Desolate but stunning."

Tom came up the steps and leant against the railing. "The story is that when George Taylor's wife Agnes died, he threw himself off the point in despair. The island was named for her." Lad had bounded over and he flopped down beside them. "George and Henry Hartwell had been disputing the name for years. He wanted Taylor Island and Henry wanted Hartwell Island, but after George died, locals settled on Agnes Island. She was the first pioneering woman to arrive here, with her stock horse and her sewing machine. Henry got the village. The rise is one of my favourite places too. A bit wild for a picnic, but a beautiful spot."

Simon came out and handed Tom a coffee. "Were you talking about a picnic?" he asked, wrapping his hands around his own mug.

"No, scenic spots on the island," said Tom, "but speaking of, I was checking the weather forecast, and the conditions are meant to be good for seeing the lights tonight."

"The aurora?" Liv squeaked, before she realised Tom was looking at Celia.

"Yeah, I, um, thought we could get a group together and go."

"That would be awesome," Celia said. "Liv? Simon?"

"Sounds good to me," Simon said.

"What sounds good?"

Liv hadn't heard Ambrose come up behind her and she felt her pulse speed up a notch.

"Tom's suggesting we go and look at the southern lights tonight," Celia told him.

"Are you sure you want everyone to come, Tom?" Ambrose asked, raising his eyebrows at Tom.

"We definitely all have to go," Celia said. "The aurora is pretty special. Has anyone seen it?"

Nobody but Tom had.

"There's no way we'll all fit in the cruiser though. Do you think Glenn might want to bring the van?" Simon said.

Celia laughed. "I imagine you can persuade him."

"Anyway," Tom said, "I ran into Gordo in town earlier and he mentioned there was a bit of an incident up here last night, so I wanted to check in."

"We had a stag group in," Ambrose said. "They're staying at the campground for the week, so you might want to keep an eye on them. Bunch of idiots."

"Ambrose was great. He calmed them down before we had to call you." Liv turned to Ambrose. "I can see you must be a good teacher." She hadn't seen him since the hot tub and she felt herself turn a bit pink, but she wasn't sure he'd heard her thank him. "Also, thanks for the hot tub, it was so relaxing." She thought of the way he'd leant in and how she'd hoped he'd kiss her. Was he wearing the same aftershave now? She was sure there was a faint whiff.

It was Tom's turn to raise his eyebrows.

Ambrose ducked his head, running his sneaker across the freshly stained wood. "It was nothing. I mean, it was a complete mess out there, so something had to be done with it."

He gave a small cough. "It's for everyone to use, even Gordo's had a go."

Liv felt like an idiot. When he'd leant over to light the candle, that must have been all he was doing.

"Well, count me in. I'm going to have a soak before our big date out," Simon said. "If you'll excuse me, I'll send Glenn a text and then I'm going to go and pick out something to wear. What colour do you think the lights are likely to be? I want to coordinate."

"Don't get your hopes up too much," Tom said. "We might not see them at all."

"And we've still got customers. Get back in the café and clear the tables." Celia sighed and pulled herself up. "Thanks, Tom, that's such a good idea. I'm looking forward to it."

After the last customers had left for the night, they hung around in the bar, waiting until close to midnight before they set off to see the lights. There was plenty of room in Glenn's van, with Simon riding up front and Celia, Tom and Malcolm squeezed into the back. Liv slid into the middle row next to Ambrose. Their legs were pressed together and she was grateful that they had two layers of denim between them. She tried to lean towards the aisle but every time they went over a bump they were jolted together and at one point hit such a big pothole they became airborne and she grabbed onto his leg by mistake.

The viewing platform was up a winding drive to the summit of the island, looking out to the south. It was cold, and Liv was glad she had bundled up. They made their way on foot along a well-maintained bush track and then switched off the torches for the last part. Liv followed closely behind Celia, who was following Tom as he led the way through the darkness. At one point, she stumbled a little and felt Ambrose's steadying hand on her elbow behind her.

Out of the bush, the night sky provided a small amount of light. A handful of locals had already gathered when they arrived, shadowy figures in the darkness. The Pansies were in a row on folding deck chairs, sharing a bottle of bubbles. Liv recognised a couple of the regulars from the bar. A woman with blue hair gave Ambrose a wave as they found a space against the railing.

Liv pulled her beanie down around her ears and waited. On the horizon, the sky was a misty, deep purple colour. Gradually she noticed a haze slowly smearing the sky with stains of pink. She snapped photos on her phone, the colours coming up in technicolour on the screen. Beside her, Simon gasped as vivid green streaks appeared, shimmering and dancing. Liv found she was speechless, feeling a bit overawed with the beauty of it. They were mostly silent, even the locals, watching as the lights played around them before fading as gradually as they'd started.

"That was incredible," she whispered, and Ambrose who was on her left murmured something she couldn't make out.

"So romantic," Simon said.

"It was pretty good," Puff said from somewhere nearby. "Not the best one I've seen."

They were the last to leave and headed back down the track, torches on so they could find their way through the bush. When they got to the van, there was no sign of Glenn. Or of Simon.

"I'll go and see where they've got to," Liv said, training her torch on the path. In the beam of her spotlight, Simon and Glenn were standing a little off the gravel track, arms entwined, snogging enthusiastically.

They broke apart when the light hit them. "Look at you lot," Simon said, "you look like stunned mullets." He took Glenn's hand and pulled him towards the van. "How quickly can you drive us back to the hotel to get rid of this lot?"

Malcolm headed inside and Tom offered to give Celia a ride home in the cruiser.

"I hope you two are going back to Glenn's house, not to mine," she said to Simon as she climbed out of the van and slid the door shut with a bang.

Liv waved them off. Ambrose was standing on the veranda, looking into the sky as though he was trying to catch a last glimpse of the aurora. She bent down to pat Mr Tiddles, who was winding around her feet hinting at a late-night snack. The cat purred loudly then sat in front of the door, lifted a paw and licked it.

"That's odd," she said. "I'm sure Mr Tiddles has never had a white paw." She stood and turned to Ambrose. "Have you noticed that?"

It felt like he was avoiding looking at her. "What? I've never really looked that closely. With my allergies. You probably just didn't notice it before." He began picking at the skin around his thumbnail.

"No, he definitely didn't. And he has a bit of white under his chin too. I know that wasn't there," she said.

There were the odd eyes too. And the fact that although the cat had been hoeing into his food, he still hadn't put on the weight he'd lost when he'd gone missing.

"If it wasn't for the collar, I'd think he was a different cat."

"I'm sure .... he's probably ..." Ambrose stuttered nervously, then sighed. He turned to face Liv, hands shoved into his pockets. "Look, I have to come clean. That's not Mr Tiddles. He's Mr Tiddles the second."

"He's what? What do you mean?"

Ambrose rested his hands on the railing and stared back out into the darkness. "I found Mr Tiddles when I was cleaning up the hot tub. He'd been dead a few days, I think. And I didn't want you to know he'd died. So I ... kind of found a replacement."

Liv felt white-hot sparks of fury shoot through her body. "So you pretended Mr Tiddles was still alive?" She felt tears forming, and ran her arm harshly across her eyes. "Why would you do that? Don't you think I deserved to know he'd died? And now you replace him thinking what, I wouldn't notice?"

"Well, to be fair, it's been almost ..."

"Don't." Her voice was dangerously low. "Don't make a joke out of this. I can't believe you've deceived me. Why? If you needed more time to come up with the money to buy me out, you could have talked to me. Or did you think I'd demand we put the hotel on the market? I'm not an unreasonable person. We could have talked about it." Her voice was bitter.

"That's not why I did it," Ambrose said, his own voice rising.

"Why then? I don't understand."

"Because I didn't want you to go," he yelled. "Okay? I didn't want you to leave."

She took a step towards him. He was looking her full in the eyes now and she felt like — what? Slapping him? She reached both hands up to either side of his face and pulled him down towards her, and kissed him.

Chapter 32

The wind started in the night, picking up in intensity until it was howling against the windows, rattling the panes. Ambrose had barely slept as it was, lying awake thinking about that kiss.

When the rain started to get serious, he gave up and got out of bed, worried that the roof might leak again. After he'd checked, relieved to see it was holding out okay, he headed into the kitchen to make himself a coffee. The lights flickered, casting eerie shadows onto the walls of the kitchen. The hotel had its own backup generator that ran the basics in case of a power failure at the island's plant and Ambrose was pleased that he'd checked it a few weeks ago. He suspected it would be needed if things got any worse.

The hotel creaked and groaned on top of the hill. Down below, the sea surged. By eight, the rain had become a torrential downpour, the streets of Hartwell struggling to cope. Malcolm came down the stairs, looking a little less put together than usual.

"That damn ferry won't be arriving any time soon, will it," he said, pouring himself a cup of coffee and looking out the window. "I've got three cases of bubbles that were supposed to come today."

"If it rains any more, the ferry jetty will be out by the front door," Gordo said, coming in the kitchen door and removing a large wet oilskin jacket. "They can pass it through the window."

Ambrose looked over and then looked again. Gordo was wearing a long nightshirt, a bit like Wee Willie Winkie if he'd been an octogenarian. That, and a pair of bright pink gumboots. His hair stood on end like he'd stuck a fork in the toaster.

"It's too bloody noisy out in that caravan," Gordo grumbled. "The rain on the aluminium makes it hard to think. I hope the whole thing doesn't take off like a kite." Outside, the noise of a siren started up. "That's not good," Gordo said, scratching at his nuts. "Might be some flooding in town. You'd better prepare for visitors."

The storm got worse and worse. Most of the main street was knee-deep in water and so was the camping ground. Howie had been ferrying people slowly up the hill all morning. It wasn't until they had half of the island squashed into the bar that Simon mentioned the stag-do guys. "Where did those idiots go?" he asked Bridie.

"They were checked in for the week," she said. "And last night they were talking about going fishing early this morning. Twistie told them not to though, since there was a storm coming." She looked a little worried. "You don't think they'd have been stupid enough to go out in this, do you?"

"I think we'd better talk to Tom," Glenn said as Twistie arrived, peeling off his slicker.

"That bloke Trevor's boat's gone from the dock," he said.

Tom called the coastguard, and radioed Weeble, then gathered up a few of the men to make a search party.

"We might need to use the hotel as a base," he told Ambrose. "The medical centre looks like it might flood, so Jackie is on her way up here with supplies."

"I'll come with you," Glenn told Tom. "We can pick Chipper up on the way too."

"Be careful, guys," Celia said, her face pale.

"You okay, Celia?" Ambrose asked.

Celia was looking at Tom as he put his coat and boots back on and Ambrose noticed she was shaking.

"Tom," she called, and he looked up. "Be careful, okay?"

Tom stopped, his hand on the door handle. He gave her a reassuring smile. "Always am," he said. "See you soon."

Olivia had taken over. She had Simon making toasted sandwiches, and a pot of soup was simmering on the stove. Bridie had been delegated to organise the back room and the pool table was stacked high with blankets and towels. The front foyer was clogged with dripping raincoats and boots. Ambrose watched as Olivia went around the room, assessing needs and checking in on families. He'd had no time to talk to her all day.

The storm was really raging, thunder and lightning striking continuously, lighting up the sky. The power went out, casting them all into gloom for a minute, then the generator kicked in. A few lights in the bar went back on, but the generator only ran the bare minimum — the kitchen fridge and chest freezer, a power bank there and the heating system. The rest of the hotel stayed dark.

"I brought up some torches from the store," Bridie said, handing them out. "And Weeble gave Howie some lanterns from the boat." She distributed them around, and Olivia handed out blankets. Ambrose went to help.

"Are you okay, Celia?" Olivia asked. Celia was standing in the office, staring out the little window at the sea. She looked a little shell-shocked. "Is it Neil?" Olivia asked. "Is this bringing back bad memories?"

"What if he dies?" Celia whispered. Ambrose and Olivia exchanged a look.

'What if who dies?' Ambrose asked.

"Tom," Celia said. "What if Tom dies and I didn't know I was in love with him, and I never tell him and he dies?"

"I think we might need a drink," Olivia said. "That's a lot

to unpack." She led Celia through to the bar kitchen and Ambrose took a bottle of whisky and poured three glasses.

"I can't believe what an idiot I've been," Celia said, sipping her drink. "All this time he was there and I didn't even realise how I felt."

"Tom is going to be fine," Olivia said, taking a sip of her own drink and pulling a face at Ambrose. "Ugh, whisky." She put her arm around Celia's shoulders. "And when he gets back, you can tell him."

"I'll have the whisky," Gordo said, "it'll warm me bones."

Olivia looked over at the cat bowl, full of biscuits. "Have you seen Mr Tiddles?" she asked Ambrose. "The second one, I mean."

Ambrose tried to read her expression in the dim light. He thought maybe she was smiling. "I hope he didn't take off outside. He might be scared."

"Who's outside?" Gordo asked?

"Mr Tiddles," Ambrose said.

"What the hell are you doing, worrying about a dead cat at a time like this?" Gordo said.

"How did you know he died?" Ambrose asked.

Gordo gave him an odd look. "Well, Howie made us have a bloody ceremony, didn't he. Laurie treated that cat like flaming royalty and Howie said we had to send him off properly. It's what Laurie would have wanted." Now it was Ambrose and Olivia's turn to look baffled.

"A ceremony for what?" Ambrose asked.

"For his funeral," Gordo said, rolling his eyes. "After Howie ran him over."

"He was already dead," Howie insisted. "I didn't kill him. Twistie put him out there while he went to get a blanket."

"What on earth are you talking about?" Ambrose said. "Mr Tiddles was alive and well when I arrived here."

Howie and Gordo looked at him and then at each other and laughed.

"That mangy old stray wasn't Mr Tiddles," Gordo said.

"Mr Tiddles was a siamese," Howie told them. "A beautiful sleek white thing. Purebred. He died not long after Laurie was taken over to the home. Didn't seem much point telling him and making him upset."

Ambrose and Olivia looked at each other in shock.

"So the whole time.." Olivia began. Overhead, there was a splintering sound, a massive crash, the sound of glass breaking and then the howling of wind, coming down the stairs.

Chapter 33

One of the old gum trees had been split in half by lightning and a huge branch had come straight through the side of the hotel, smashing the window in the honeymoon suite. Rain was pouring in, soaking the new carpet.

Simon and Liv struggled with the huge bed, pulling it across the room to keep it away from the gaping hole. The picture above the bed had fallen off and part of a branch had ripped the canvas. Liv threw it on top of the bed and then went to try to dislodge the branch, her shoes crushing through broken glass.

Ambrose came back with a tarpaulin and Liv's toolbox and the three of them tried pushing the branch out of the hole it had created, the rain sleeting in on them in sharp needles, wind howling.

"I think we might be better to pull the whole thing in," Ambrose suggested, his hair dripping and his shirt soaked.

Howie and Gordo came up the stairs in their raincoats, flashlights scanning across the room, and between them all they managed to yank the large branch inside. They boarded up the hole with a piece of gib, tarp and nails. It was keeping the rain out, at least for now.

"I'll get the broom," Gordo offered. "Sweep up some of this glass."

"I've got some old towels in the boot," Howie said. "They might soak up some of the water on the carpet."

Ambrose wrung the water from the bottom of his shirt. "Let's get out of these wet clothes, shall we?" and Liv's mind went to him, standing naked in the shower, droplets of water running down his chest and …

"Liv?" Simon said, and she shook herself back into the present.

"Right, yes, good idea." She looked over at Ambrose, her cheeks feeling flushed. "Shit, you've cut your hand," she said. Watery pink rivulets were running down Ambrose's wrist, staining the cuff of his sleeve.

"It's fine, I just nicked it on the glass edge," Ambrose said. But Liv's head was fuzzy and then things went black.

When she came to, she was on her bed and Jackie was there, Ambrose hovering behind her, his hand wrapped in a bandage.

"You're fine, darl, you fainted, but you're okay," Jackie said. "Lie there for a minute and don't try to jump up." Jackie popped a pillow under her feet and gave them a reassuring rub.

"Sorry," Liv said. "I don't do well with blood. How embarrassing."

"Honestly, I'm pleased to discover you have a fault." Ambrose smiled. "I was starting to think you were too perfect."

"Shall we get you out of your wet clothes, hun?" Jackie said, and Ambrose cleared his throat.

"Right, I'll go, leave you to it. I should get changed too." He shut the door behind him and Jackie sighed.

"Isn't he lovely," she said, helping Liv sit up slowly. "It was rather romantic the way he scooped you up and carried you in here. Like *An Officer and a Gentleman*. If I was ten years younger, I'd snap that man up, I tell you."

Rugged up in a pair of track pants and a jumper, Liv headed gingerly down the stairs and back to the bar, as Glenn came in the door.

"They've found the boat," he said. "They're all seasick and cold, but otherwise fine. Tom's bringing them up now."

"Well, now that is good news," Gordo said. "I think that deserves a drink."

Liv suspected he'd have had one if the news had been bad too, but she let it go.

"I'll have a red wine," she told him. "Anyone else?"

Simon helped Gordo pour drinks for anyone wanting one

and they all raised their glasses in cheers. "Thank you so much for all your help." Liv smiled at everyone, thinking how nice it was to know them all, and how much she would miss them if she went.

"Ah, no trouble," Howie said.

"Many hands make light work, as our old mate Smudge used to say," Gordo added, and then he and Howie clinked glasses. "To Smudge," they both said before sipping their drinks, seeming to have momentarily forgotten their feud. Liv had no idea who Smudge was.

Ambrose had changed into a warm jumper and jeans and Liv looked at him over her drink. He seemed so different now to the man she had met at the funeral. So much more content. He suited living here on Aggie, like he had found his place. She wondered if maybe she had too.

Tom came in the front door, the stag-do guys trailing in behind him looking subdued and miserable.

"Any chance this lot could have a couple of rooms tonight?" he asked as he hung up his jacket, his face ruddy from the wind. "I'm sure they'd be willing to pay summer rates."

A door banged and then Celia came flying out of the back room, barrelling over to Tom.

"Hey Celia—" he said but then she was kissing him, long and deep like there was no one in the room but the two of them. Tom's eyes went wide and then he was all in, pulling her into him. The whole room let out a collective sigh.

Eventually they pulled apart. Tom looked like he thought he might be dreaming.

"I love you, Tom Williams," Celia said.

"I love you too," Tom said, grinning widely, and everyone clapped, like they were watching a movie.

Chapter 34

The power was back on and the storm seemed to be letting up. Liv checked the stag-do guys into their rooms and made sure there were plenty of spare towels in the showers. Their belongings were at the campground, probably under water, so she offered them the use of the washing machines and dryers.

"Thanks for your hospitality," one of the men said. "We really appreciate it, don't we lads?"

Trevor looked contrite. "Sorry I was such a dick the other night. You could have kicked us out on our arses and you haven't. If there's anything we can do …?"

"If you're handy with a chainsaw, we've got a tree that needs to be cut up, when the weather clears," Liv said. "I'll get some food sent up to your rooms."

"Thanks, and happy to help with the tree, and anything else you need done."

Liv checked that the patched-up window in the honeymoon suite was holding out. The room looked like a bomb had gone off. There was less than a week before the gallery opening and she'd need to get the window pane repaired, dry the carpet and repaint where the fallen tree had damaged the windowsill. They had a full house and the room was booked for two nights for the exhibition, and giving the Minister for the Arts her shabby room as an alternative was not an option. She tried not to feel too disheartened.

Downstairs, Celia was distributing bowls of fries and toasted sandwiches to anyone who was still holed up in the hotel. Ambrose, with the help of Sandra Banks, had organised a board games tournament for the kids in the back room. Simon was teaching Sandra's youngest, Benji, how to play poker.

"Where's Tom?" Liv asked Celia, following her back into the kitchen to give her a hand. Celia lifted a basket of fries from the fryer and gave it a shake. Liv pinched a large one from the top and blew on it before taking a bite. It felt like hours since she'd eaten anything and it was crispy and delicious. Celia shook some of the fries into a bowl, added some salt and handed them to Liv.

"Here, eat these. Jackie said you were feeling a bit faint before." She pushed over a squeezy bottle of tomato sauce and Liv caught it before it fell off the bench. "Tom and Glenn went to check in on everyone. It looks like the lowest part of the village is the most affected, but he wanted to make sure everyone living up in the hills was okay as well." Celia's face broke out in a smile when she said Tom's name.

"So all this time, you've been harbouring a secret crush?" Liv teased.

"Turns out we both have. The thought of him dying was a massive wake-up call. I've always thought he was a lovely guy. He was there for me when Neil died, and he's amazing with everyone on the island." She laughed and ran a hand across her hair. "I wasn't aware though that it wasn't part of his duties to pop into the hotel a couple of times every day."

"You thought he visited everyone daily?"

"No, I thought because it was a hotel he was checking on the visitors, or making sure nobody was driving home drunk." She'd finished plating up the chips and removed the toasted sandwiches from the machine. "Here, take these out to the kids and stop asking me so many questions."

Some of the villagers had returned to their houses but a few who lived right in town were staying in the hotel for the night. Malcolm was due to fly off the island the following day to collect the paintings and was nursing a large brandy, fretting to Howie about the opening. Howie had returned from dropping a load of locals home and Liv handed them one of the bowls of fries she was carrying.

"Thanks for your taxi service, Howie," she said. "Can I get you a drink? On the house, of course."

"Glad to help. That's what it's like on Aggie, everyone chips in when they're needed. There will be a lot of clean-up around the island, and we'll all pitch in to get it done." He patted her arm. "Don't worry, everything will be shipshape for the big opening. I'll have a small raspberry and lemonade, if you wouldn't mind."

Gordo had fallen asleep at the bar, which was no surprise. He'd worked as hard as anyone, settling people in and handing out blankets, serving drinks and helping Celia with the food. He'd let Declan and James pull a couple of pints while Tom hadn't been there to see, much to their delight. She poured Howie's drink and served Puff and Alan Banks, before giving Gordo a nudge. He'd done enough for the day.

He was sound asleep and didn't budge. "Gordo, why don't you head out now," Liv said. She gently shook his arm, then a little more firmly. When he still didn't move, Liv leant down closer. "Gordo," she said a little louder.

It dawned on her that he wasn't snoring. Liv patted Gordo's hand gently. It felt cool to the touch. She called Jackie, who was sitting with Tina's youngest on her knee.

"Jackie," she whispered when she came over. "I think Gordo has passed away."

Chapter 35

The day they flew Gordo off the island was clear and crisp. It was hard to believe there had been a massive storm, aside from the odd fallen branch and the big puddles that still remained around the township. Everyone had come out in force the next day to begin the tidy-up. The school was closed and even the smallest of the students was helping.

On the night of the storm, Tom had returned to his house next to the police station and picked up the casket he kept stored there. Ambrose remembered Gordo telling Olivia about it, after the fire at the school.

The pub had fallen silent as they'd carried him out. Because the medical centre was still under threat of flooding, Tom had taken Gordo in the back of the police cruiser to the station for the night.

At one o'clock, Ambrose made his way to the veranda, where Olivia and Howie were already waiting. Malcolm came down from his room, and Celia and Simon from the kitchen. There was the distant thrum of an engine and then the plane came into view, flying low over the island. Flumes of condensation trailed behind as the little Cherokee circled overhead and then grew smaller as it disappeared around the island for Gordo's final lap.

Malcolm had removed his hat and had it pressed to his chest. Howie lifted his hand in a wave. "See you, my old mate," he said, pulling out a checked handkerchief and blowing his nose furiously.

They stood in silence for a while, each with their own thoughts. Gordo had been a staple on Aggie as long as Ambrose had been coming there. He and Mike had once broken a pool cue and were too scared to admit it to Laurie. Gordo had glued it up and hung it back in the rack. "Good as new," he'd said with a wink. He'd turned a blind eye when he'd caught them taking sneaky sips of Laurie's beer and taught them how to play gin rummy one wet afternoon when they'd had nothing better to do.

They stood until the plane came into view again, reached the village and then headed out to sea.

"Let's open the bar," Ambrose said. His voice was a little rough. Olivia wiped her eyes with the sleeve of her sweatshirt. "I think we could all use a drink."

Later that afternoon, Ambrose found Oliva in the honeymoon suite, cleaning up the debris from the storm. There were three fan heaters on low and she was vigorously sweeping up leaves and twigs with an outdoor broom. Some of the hair from her ponytail had escaped and one strand was stuck to the side of her face. Ambrose wondered how he'd ever thought she was a princess. He'd never seen anyone work as hard as Olivia had, to get the hotel ready.

"Can I help?" he asked, causing Olivia to jump and almost hit herself in the face with the broom handle.

"Um, yeah, sure. Thanks. Could you put this pile into that garden bag over there?"

"Sorry that your hard work has been ruined," he said, scooping up a handful of leaves. "It's looking good though, you've really done a great job."

Olivia sighed and straightened, leaning on the broom and resting one hand on the curve of her back. "This room's not as bad as it looks. Gavin says he's got some glass panels in his workshop and apparently Chipper isn't bad at glass installation." She laughed. "I'll have to take his word for that. Actually, once Greta left and he stopped moping around, he really got stuck in. I couldn't have done all this without him."

"None of it would have been done without you," Ambrose said, feeling awkward and thinking about the kiss the other night. With everything that had happened, they still hadn't talked about it.

"I know you've been working hard too, keeping the hotel ticking over, and paying for the materials. Sorry if I implied you haven't been doing your share." Olivia sat down on the edge of the bed, which was ridiculously large, and picked up the picture that had fallen from the wall.

"Do you think we could persuade Malcolm to paint something to replace this?"

Ambrose studied the freshly painted wall. "It definitely needs something. Could we hang that up again in the meantime? So it doesn't look so bare."

"It's got a bit of storm damage," Olivia said, picking at the top of the canvas that had started to come away. There was something underneath, but it wasn't blank like Ambrose had expected.

"That's weird," Oliva mused, as she pulled a neat strip from the canvas.

"You won't be able to hang it up if you pull it apart like that," Ambrose said.

"I think … it's been covered over with another canvas. It looks like there's another picture underneath this one."

Carefully she peeled more of the picture away. They stood staring at the canvas in awe.

"The sneaky bugger," Ambrose said.

Now that the outer layer had been pulled away, Ambrose could see the muted colours of another painting. The murky green background contrasted with Ida's skin, her head was slightly bent, hair concealing her face, with streaks of purple and gold highlighting the voluptuousness of her breasts. Her legs were crossed, hands clasped loosely in her lap, allowing no more than a hint of her nakedness beneath them. Laurie's double L looped signature graced the bottom. Olivia hung the painting back on the cheap plastic hook, and they stood back to get a better look.

"So that's what Laurie meant by the nude being under wraps," Olivia said. Her head was tilted slightly to one side and she had an expression Ambrose couldn't read. "Isn't it beautiful? I can see why the art world went crazy when he first showed it. You definitely feel something, looking at this."

"It really is striking. Ida was clearly a good subject, but the way that Laurie's painted her, there's something that makes you ..." He looked over at Olivia.

"Horny?" she said.

Their eyes met for a second. Hers seemed even greener against the dull background of the painting. In a beat they moved towards each other and Ambrose felt the coolness of Liv's hands as they snaked under his jumper. He kissed her, and it was twice as much as the kiss in the doorway had been. Liv pulled her sweatshirt over her head, further dislodging the hair from her ponytail and then pulled Ambrose down onto the bed in a hot tangled mess.

🐾

"What are we going to do with the portrait?" he said later. The air felt cool against his bare skin, despite the warmth of Liv's body curled against his. He reached down and grabbed the quilt from the floor and pulled it over them.

Liv craned her neck to look at the painting hanging on the wall. "It's quite inspiring. Could we keep it?"

Ambrose laughed and ran a hand under the blanket, resting it on Liv's hip. "It might be too distracting if we want to get this room fixed up by Friday."

"And Chipper will be here, doing the window," Liv added. She snuggled closer to Ambrose and he thought he'd like to stay there with her for days.

"We should give it to Erina," he said after a bit. "She made a promise to Ida to find the painting and now it should belong to her."

"You're right." Liv lifted her head from where it had been resting on Ambrose's chest and kissed him. "But while we've got it here, what say we ..."

Ambrose rolled her onto her back and returned the kiss.

Chapter 36

Erina had been thrilled to receive the painting, so Liv was surprised to see her back the day before the exhibition with it tucked under her arm. She asked if Liv and Ambrose would come out to the studio with Malcolm so she could talk to them.

"I wanted to read you something," she said, pulling out a battered envelope. "I've been reading those letters of Kuia's and I think maybe she would want the nude in the exhibition after all."

Laurie, my love,

Thank you, darling, for buying back the painting. I'm grateful to you for retrieving it. I was probably a little harsh to you when you exhibited it, but I was rather shocked. I know you can't see my face, but I felt like everyone would know it was me.

I imagine, when I'm eighty, wrinkled and contentedly

rotund, that I'll be proud to have been your muse, and wish you could show me to the world. Do you imagine we will still be doing this in our eighties, my lover?

But for now, while Charles and I are still married, and with Teressa so little, I'd rather that piece be for your eyes only. I have missed you intensely while Charles has been home so long over winter. I long to be with you again, my sweet.

Until then,
ever yours,
Ida

Erina handed the painting over to Malcolm.

"It would make an amazing addition to the exhibition," Liv said, "but are you sure?"

Erina nodded. "It would be a loan, of course, but I talked to Mum and she gave her blessing." She gave Malcolm an apologetic grin. "It's not framed, sorry."

"Never mind that, this is wonderful," Malcolm said. "I think we could make this the centrepiece of the whole exhibition, maybe put it up on the mezzanine by itself as the final stop on the way around." He had arrived back from Auckland the day before with the framed pictures and it was the first time Liv had seen them displayed. They looked brilliant.

"She's all yours," Erina said.

"My God, it really does invoke such a feeling of eroticism,"

Malcolm said, studying the painting. Liv did a quick glance over at Ambrose who caught her eye and then looked away, a faint blush and a grin on his face.

Celia lent Liv her car and she arrived at the ferry terminal a little early. Sean had replied enthusiastically to her invitation to attend the gallery opening and Liv was grateful to have his support and looking forward to seeing him. She'd sent an invitation to Deirdre and to Warren and Laura, but hadn't been surprised when they'd declined, so it would be extra nice to have a friend there. The media attention wouldn't hurt either, as long as it wasn't on her, and she planned to avoid the cameras.

Liv watched as the ferry chugged slowly through the harbour. It seemed like forever ago that she'd been on that boat herself, seasick and apprehensive. The island had seemed so tiny and remote and she had thought it wouldn't have anything to offer. How unenlightened she had been. Aggie offered so much more than fancy stores and exotic restaurants. There were no fast cars — in fact, hardly any cars at all — and no hustle and bustle, and once Liv had got to know everyone, she never felt lonely here. It was funny how you could live in a big city surrounded by people and feel like you were invisible. Now, if she wanted someone to talk to, she had Celia and Simon, or she could call in to see Kate at the library. She could chat to Bridie at the store, stop for a word with Tom when she ran into him in the street, or Glenn or Jackie or Tina. Of course there were the customers in the pub and the quiz night, funny old Howie … and there had been Gordo. And Ambrose.

It wasn't only Ambrose who had made the way she felt about Agnes Island shift; that had been gradually happening without her realising, but since their honeymoon suite tryst, she had been daydreaming about what it would be like to stay permanently.

Weeble secured the ferry to the dock and Liv got out of the car and made her way down the jetty. A group of teenagers, headed home from boarding school for the weekend, got off first, chattering loudly, and then Sean hopped off, an expensive-looking leather tote bag slung over his shoulder and carrying a small tube.

"Livvy." He pulled her into a warm embrace. "This place looks absolutely stunning. Why have I not been here before?"

"Because it's a national secret," Liv said, extracting herself from where she had burrowed into his cream puffer jacket. "I hope you've brought some country clothes with you."

"Other than my glad rags for the opening, it's all tracksuits and runners, babe."

The teenagers from the boat were dispersing in various directions. "Doesn't look like you had them fan-girling over you on the ride over."

Sean laughed. "I doubt very much they had any idea who I was. I must be old and obsolete."

Weeble came over and shook Sean's hand. "Pleasure to have you on board, Mr Anthony, sorry it wasn't the smoothest ride."

Liv bit back a giggle.

"I have sturdy sealegs, my man," Sean said. They watched as Weeble made his bowlegged way into the passenger terminal. "Karen sends her apologies and her love, by the way. It was a bit of a mission with a new baby and the two rugrats. Bloody hell, sometimes I feel like we're too old to be doing the baby thing all over again."

"How is Sinclair? He looks adorable." Liv waited while Sean extracted his bag from the luggage hold.

"Here, this is for you, at your request," he said, handing her the tube. "Sinclair is wonderful. Colicky, but cute." He extended the handle of his bag and they headed up the dock, wheels clacking unevenly against the wooden slats.

Liv opened the door to Celia's little hatchback.

"Is this your car? Did you leave it unlocked?" Sean hoisted the bag into the boot.

Liv laughed. "Nobody locks anything on Aggie. And this is my friend Celia's car. She's the chef at the hotel. Wait until you try her pappardelle al cinghiale. It's as good as anything you'd get in Tuscany."

He got into the passenger seat and Liv started the car. "Also, don't go all diva on me when you find out you haven't got the best room in the house. It's very simple and we've been doing it up on a budget."

"You know I don't care about all that stuff, Livvy-Lou." He was gazing out the window as the car chugged along the main road, past the garage and the store. "I'm going to have to film something down here. I can see why the old man raved about it. I could follow in his footsteps."

Simon came rushing down the steps to help with the bags as they pulled up at the hotel. Sean unfurled his long legs from the little car and stared out across the harbour. "This view is out of this world."

"I can't believe it, Sean Anthony in the flesh, well, unfortunately with a shirt on," Simon gushed as he took Sean's tote from him, leaving him to carry the heavier bag.

Liv found herself eager for Sean to meet Ambrose, curious to know what he would think of him, but Ambrose was nowhere to be seen.

"The bathrooms are shared," Simon prattled, as he followed them up the stairs to the rooms. "And there's a hot tub out the back. Let Ambrose know if you'd like to use it and he'll fire it up. I'm available if you need your back scrubbed."

"You're a shameless flirt, Simon," Liv said. "I'll leave you to get settled, Sean. I've got to open up the bar. I've been brushing up my hospo skills since our long-time barkeep passed away recently." She felt a lump form in her throat as she said it.

"I'll go have a nosy around and join you shortly," Sean said.

Liv went down to open up the bar, expecting that half the town would show up to meet the great Sean Anthony.

At least, those old enough to know who he was.

Chapter 37

"Were you in love with Connor?" Ambrose asked Liv as they lay in the hot tub soaking. He regretted the question as soon as it came out, nervous of the answer, but Liv just laughed.

"No, not even a bit," she told him, pressing her long legs up against his as she shifted slightly. "And I don't think he loved me either. He just saw me as a good fit for him. He used to call me his talisman and I honestly think he believed I was good luck. But he barely knew me, and we really didn't have much in common. I just got myself into something and it snowballed until it was hard to extract myself."

"Well, I'm rather glad you did," he said.

"Me too," Liv said, rolling over to face him and sloshing water over the edge of the tub. She traced a finger along his lip and Ambrose's heart thudded heavily in his chest. "After tomorrow we might have to put a hold on these baths," she said, leaning in to kiss him. "The naked part at least anyway."

"Well, we'd better make the most of this one then," he said, kissing her back.

Malcolm had arranged for media and art critics and a couple of other well-known artists to be part of the big unveiling and the hotel was at full occupancy. He'd insisted on getting them to the island a day early in case the weather turned on them, so Ambrose had spent the entire day yesterday on the golf cart Declan had managed to get running, going backwards and forwards from the wharf to the hotel to the airstrip.

His phone rang as he got out of the shower the next morning and he looked at the caller ID with surprise.

"Hello, Mum," he said, "is something wrong?"

"Darling," Claudette laughed. "Can't a mother call her son just because?" Ambrose waited. "Good news, however," she said. "I've juggled my schedule and I'm coming to visit. I'm headed to the airport now. I should land on the island at one thirty."

"You're coming to Aggie?" he said. 'Today?"

"Well, of course, darling, I want to be there to support you and your exhibition." Ambrose could hear her writing, the pen scratching against paper." Joan tells me *News Today* is covering it, and I do feel that it would be good to get the constituents onboard with my policies there."

"Right," Ambrose said. Of course, that was why Claudette was coming now. It made for good press. "You might want to avoid mentioning your anti-gun stance here," he told her. "There are a lot of hunters."

"Excellent, good to know." Claudette called something out to Joan and there was murmuring in the background. "I must go, darling, see you soon."

The ceremony began at two, but there had been a lot going on all day to prepare for it and Ambrose had barely had time to change into his suit and tie. There had been no time to talk to Olivia at all that day, but she had been on his mind the whole time.

Malcolm's bubbles had arrived and had been chilled down. Trays of flutes had been placed on tables with white table-cloths, ready for the opening speeches. A red ribbon had been erected across the studio door, to be cut by the mayor. Celia had done a brilliant job with breakfast and was now preparing canapes to serve, Simon critiquing as they went.

Inside, the studio looked incredible. The art was displayed showing Ida from older to younger, the final piece being the nude. It took the viewer on a path back in time. Forget-me-nots in rustic vases sat next to strategically placed seats for taking in Lawrence Lloyd's incredible talent. A large black and white photo of Laurie sat on an easel by the door.

A local elder from the island's marae had been asked to perform a karakia, and Erina welcomed guests with the mihi whakatau.

Claudette arrived with her own press, getting off the plane in a cloud of perfume and air hugs. She was busy networking and Ambrose watched her with grim amusement as she played her part.

Olivia's actor friend was here too, causing a bit of a stir. Jackie and Bridie had both brought autograph books for him to sign. He was graciously posing for photos, all smiles.

Declan and James took turns running visitors up in the golf buggy from two charter boats Malcolm had hired to bring guests over from the mainland, and Glenn brought up the surplus in the van.

"Appreciate your help, buddy," Ambrose said as Glenn brought the last lot up and deposited them in the garden not long before the ceremony was due to start.

Glenn grabbed a champagne flute off Simon as he flitted past, giving him a cheeky wink. "No trouble, mate, I've got full tours for the next couple of days from the hotel guests, so I'm a happy man."

Olivia came out of the front door and Ambrose felt like someone had hit him with a cattle prod. She was in a forest-green dress that clung to her body, her hair up in a fancy bun thing. She had on makeup and heels and she was a vision. Ambrose wished that he could paint like Laurie and capture her in the moment. He wanted to keep this image of her in his mind until he was a very old man. Wanted to see her grow old, like Laurie had done with Ida.

"Well, don't you look ravishing?" Sean said, giving her

a kiss, and Ambrose's fists curled at his sides, his stomach knotting. Olivia smiled and asked Simon to take their picture. "I knew you were the right woman for the job," Sean said, "already working on my PR and without leaving the island."

"That one is *not* going on social media," Liv said. "It's for Karen. But we should get some shots of you with the mayor and with Claudette too."

"What job is this?" Simon asked.

"Livvy has agreed to do my PR for me now that I've gotten out of my old contract," Sean said. "She's going to set up her own exclusive firm, aren't you, Livvy?"

"Ambrose, it's time to get started," Malcolm said, but Ambrose could hardly hear him. Olivia was leaving? Going back to her old life and her old job? Just like that? Was she even planning to tell him? Now that Mr Tiddles wasn't holding them back from selling, it seemed she was ready to leave. Leave the hotel and the island and him. It wasn't like she'd ever given any indication that she might stay, but over the last few days, Ambrose had been hopeful. That maybe she had changed her mind.

He could feel a lump rising in his throat. This was why he never looked for relationships. Why he was better on his own. His mother had shipped him off to boarding school, and all the women he had dated had been more interested in the son of a politician than a mere school teacher. He never seemed to learn.

He cleared his throat, going over to Malcolm and standing by his side. The cameras flashed, and Ambrose put on the smile that Claudette had taught him, hardening his heart while he did it.

Chapter 38

The exhibition was amazing. Malcolm had deemed it 'the art event of the year' and Liv could see from the faces of all the guests that he had been right — people loved it and they would come to Agnes Island to see Laurie's work. Things could not be better for the hotel.

Sean had offered Liv a contract, doing his PR. He had a new film lined up for the new year, several brand contracts and the possibility of a hosting job on a new TV series. But the best part was she could do it all remotely. It would bring in some much-needed extra income for her too.

He'd also brought over a request for Liv. When she'd heard about Sean's dad filming on Aggie, and how Ambrose had loved it as a kid, she had asked Sean if there was any chance his father Tad would sign an autograph for Ambrose. Tad had gone one better, finding an old promotional poster of the movie and signing that. Liv couldn't wait to give it to Ambrose once the excitement of the exhibition had died down.

She was so proud of how the hotel looked now. It still needed more doing to it, but it was vastly improved from when she had arrived all those months ago. It turned out that inheriting the Hartwell Hotel had been exactly what she needed. A distraction from all the drama, but also a chance to reset and look at what she really wanted in her life.

She wasn't a city girl. She'd done it, but it wasn't who she really was. She knew that now. She loved living on Aggie and, she realised, she might just love Ambrose too.

He was kind and gentle and clever and gorgeous and every time she saw him, her breath caught a little and she got butterflies. It was early days in their relationship, but she felt like she'd gotten to know him so well since they'd taken over the hotel.

That, and the sex had been pretty damned inspiring. Especially for a first try. The second had been even better. She'd stayed in Ambrose's room the last two nights and the chemistry was definitely there. Yes, Liv could definitely love Ambrose. And she thought maybe he might feel the same.

Claudette was standing with Ambrose on the front veranda, posing for yet another photo, this time with her son. Most of the exhibition guests had gone, some taking the last ferry or the return charter boats and others into the bar for dinner. Most of the locals had gone home, preferring to avoid the tourists where they could. Liv waited until the cameraman was done, then headed up the steps to meet Ambrose's mother.

"Claudette, I'm Liv," she said, extending her hand. "It's nice to finally meet you."

Claudette shook her hand firmly, then looked at Ambrose.

"Olivia is the other half-owner of the hotel for the meantime," he said, and Claudette gave Liv a faint smile.

"Yes, of course, so nice to meet you," she said. "Ambrose and I were just discussing how charming the place is, weren't we, darling?"

"Well, I won't interrupt," Liv said. "I only wanted to say that I've had a clean-up and put fresh sheets on my bed, so I'm happy for you to take my room tonight. I'm sorry we can't offer you a proper room."

Claudette's eyebrows rose. "And where would you sleep?" she asked drily.

"Umm, with Ambrose?" Liv felt like she had put her foot in it somehow. Ambrose wasn't even looking at her, and the vibe she was getting was frosty. She had no idea why, but it was probably way too early to reveal to his mother that they had a relationship. "Or with Celia," she added awkwardly.

"That's kind, but I won't be staying," Claudette said. "I have Nigel on standby, ready to go."

"Okay, well, we appreciate your coming." Liv wasn't sure what else to say, so she left them to it, going inside to change. Only she'd forgotten her handbag, she realised. She was out of the habit of locking her room, but after she'd packed up her things and tucked them in the corner of the upstairs lounge, she'd made her room look as bare and as much like a hotel room as possible, thinking she would lock it and give the key to Claudette. She had put the key in her handbag, which she seemed to remember putting down in the office of the studio.

She headed back outside through the restaurant door and that was when she heard Claudette.

"I do hope you're not serious about this Olivia girl," she said. "I recognised her at once, of course, with all that mess concerning Connor Reed. She really isn't the sort of girl to get serious about, darling."

Liv froze, not wanting to listen, but unable to help herself.

"Of course not," Ambrose said. "It was only a fling. Olivia will be heading back to the mainland and I'll buy her out. It's nothing for you to be concerned about."

Liv crept back inside, handbag forgotten.

She went into the office and shut the door, standing in the dark, her hand on her chest. It was hard to catch her breath. Outside, she could hear laughter and music coming from the bar and she cried silently, her life upended once again.

The door opened and Simon put his hand around the corner, turning on the light.

"Liv, what's wrong, hun?" he asked.

The next morning, after a long night crying on Simon's shoulder, Liv got on the first ferry, snivelling into Sean's puffer the whole way back to the mainland, with no idea what she was going to do when she got there.

Chapter 39

Ambrose had stayed in the bar drinking with Glenn long after everyone else had gone to bed. He kept expecting to see Olivia but she didn't make an appearance all night, so he'd acted as barkeep and been on a high with praise for the hotel, the exhibition and the island itself from the guests. When he finally stumbled into his room, he thought he might find her in his bed, or that she'd come in later to find him, but he'd slept alone, his plan to confront her about leaving delayed, which was perhaps a good thing given his sobriety — or lack thereof.

He slept late and woke up feeling crappy, lying in bed for a while, stewing over the fact that Olivia was planning to leave and hadn't even mentioned it. He wondered when she would bother to tell him. A shower and painkillers barely touched the sides of his hangover and eventually he headed to the kitchen needing something greasy. Celia was in there, vigorously mopping the floor. She glanced up at him, then went back to mopping, her mouth set in a straight line.

"Simon has dropped off a couple of the guests to the airstrip since you were nowhere to be seen this morning," she said, sniffing. "I don't know what happened last night, but Liv has left you something in the office." Her eyes were red and she seemed upset for some reason, so Ambrose quickly grabbed a coffee and a pastry and left her alone.

There was a cardboard tube on his desk and a letter with his name on it. He opened the envelope first.

Ambrose

Thanks for the 'fling'. I'll arrange for my share of the hotel to be transferred to your name. It's obvious to me that it should always have been yours, and I don't want anything for it. I'm sorry things didn't work out better, but I wish you well. Hope you enjoy the gift.

Olivia

Ambrose read the letter several times, trying to work it out. Why was she giving her share of the hotel to him? And why were there quotation marks around the word fling? She was the one who planned to leave him and go back to her old life. It had hardly been a mere fling to him.

Inside the tube was a poster. He unrolled it carefully and saw that it was from the Tad Chadwick movie filmed on Aggie. It was even signed. Even more confused, he headed back to find Celia.

"Have you seen Olivia around? I need to talk to her."

Celia glared at him. "She's gone, Ambrose," she said. "She took the ferry back this morning."

"What? She left already? What did she say? Was she with Sean?"

"Well, yes," Celia said. "She asked me to look after Mr Tiddles and said she was going to miss me. I couldn't get much out of her, but she was crying."

"Crying? Why was she crying?"

"I don't know! Maybe because she didn't want to go and she's heartbroken?" Celia yelled.

"Heartbroken?" Ambrose scoffed. "She was planning to go all along. She's got a new job with Sean and she was leaving anyway. Not that she'd bothered to tell me."

Celia looked at him for a beat, then shook her head. "Oh, Ambrose," she said quietly. "What have you done?"

"Me?" Ambrose said. "I'm not the one who's left!"

"The job was remote," Simon said from the doorway. "Liv had no intention of leaving."

Ambrose turned to look at him, his heart pounding in his chest. "What? No. She ..." He paused, trying to think. Had Olivia been planning to stay? Then why leave now? "Then why has she gone?" he asked, his voice strained.

"She heard you talking to your mother last night," Simon said. "And she got the message loud and clear."

Ambrose thought back to what he'd said to Claudette. He'd been so angry that Olivia was planning to go and he'd brushed off his feelings for her, afraid of being hurt again. His stomach sank.

She didn't answer her phone. He tried texting and it came back undelivered. He searched futilely for her on social media. He rang again and again, suspecting she had blocked his number.

He'd royally screwed up, he realised.

Four days later he was feeling miserable with guilt and still trying to get hold of Olivia. He'd tried everything he could to find out where she was. It wasn't until a package arrived from her mother that he had some hope. There was a return address on the box and now he at least had a starting point.

He forced himself to get through the school week, distracted and apprehensive. On Friday afternoon he stood in the staffroom, staring out at the harbour. The weather had turned awful, a spring storm brewing. Choppy waves splashed up onto the dock, causing the seagulls that had been hanging around to fly off in a rage. There was no sign of the ferry.

"Doesn't look like the ferry's coming in today," Maron said, coming up behind him. "I was expecting some supplies from the MOE. Looking at that sky, Nigel won't be flying either. Go home and hunker down for the weekend, Ambrose."

He stopped in at the shop on his way home, needing some more cat food for Mr Tiddles the third. The cat had taken to wandering into Ambrose's room in the small hours of the morning and attacking Ambrose as he slept, something Ambrose was sure was a pointed commentary on the absence of Olivia and the reminder that it was his fault.

Bridie was at the door, shaking out an umbrella when he arrived, her ample bottom squeezed into what Ambrose was ninety percent sure was a pair of Juicy track pants that Olivia had discarded.

"Hello, love," Bridie said, giving him a smile. "You're just in time. I've just closed up over at the post office. No seeds for Lester today again, sorry." Ambrose shook the rain off his jacket before following her inside. "I suppose you've seen the article?" she added as Ambrose headed towards the back aisle for cat biscuits.

"Which article is that?" he called back, grabbing the cat food.

"The one about Liv and her old beau," Bridie said, pulling an apron over her head. "That Connor bloke. He's desperate to get her back apparently, says she was his lucky charm." She tied up the apron strings behind her back. "Ohh, do you think that's why she went back then?" She pointed to the counter where the local newspaper and a couple of magazines were spread out. On the front cover of one was a photo of Connor Reed in his All Blacks uniform, kneeling on the pitch holding a ring box, with the title 'Come back to me, Lucky Liv' across the top. "He says he plans to woo her back," Bridie added helpfully. "They've lost every game since she turned him down, you know."

Ambrose felt a bit sick. He stood looking at the glossy magazine cover, his heart sinking. He added a chocolate bar, a pack of gum and then, as Bridie started to ring him up, he slid the magazine across to her.

"May as well have that too," he said casually. "For Simon."

"Of course, love," Bridie said, entering his total into the eftpos machine. He swiped his card and she handed him his bag. "She'd be a fool to take him back," she added softly, her voice laced with sympathy. "I've always said, you can never trust a good-looking man."

The rain started bucketing down and the wind had amped up by the time he reached the top of the hill. For the first time since he'd arrived on Aggie, the hotel didn't feel like home. All he wanted to was to find Olivia and beg her to come back, but there was no way off the island.

Chapter 40

It wasn't only Ambrose who was miserable that weekend. The weather didn't let up and there was concern that they'd be in for another big storm like they'd had earlier in the month.

Without Olivia there he had to double up on bar duty, even though only a few hardy locals came out in the storm. Ambrose found himself listening to Puff and Weeble droning on about the great white they'd caught the previous year until he wanted to yell at them to go home.

Both Celia and Simon gave him the cold shoulder, only speaking to him if they had to.

Whenever the door to the bar opened, Ambrose looked up hopefully, but of course it was never Olivia. There was no way off the island, and there was also no way onto it, but there was zero chance she'd change her mind and come back anyway.

"Mate." Glenn had hung his dripping rain jacket on the hook by the door and taken off his gumboots before he padded over to the bar in his socks. "I could do with a beer. I've spent the entire day doing paperwork and it's really not my thing."

Ambrose wordlessly poured him a pint and pushed it over.

Glenn was leaning on the bar, looking a bit put upon. "Simon has asked me to ask you if you want to put an order in for a roast lamb dinner tonight." Glenn grimaced. "He said they could probably spare you a meal, and that you're lucky it's quiet because you'd be low priority otherwise." He took a sip of his beer. "Crikey, this feels like passing notes in primary school. Hopefully we're not going to have another Gordo/Howie situation and someone will still be acting as go-between for the two of you in another thirty years."

"Do you really think Simon will be on the island for that long?" Ambrose asked, aware he was being rancorous. "Most people don't stay, do they?"

Glenn seemed unperturbed. "You are though, aren't you? Even if you did screw up your chance at happiness."

They glowered at each other until Ambrose turned away. "How was I to know she wasn't planning on leaving?"

"Ever heard of a thing called communication? If you didn't tell her how you were feeling, how could you expect her to know it was more than a fling?"

"I didn't know she was thinking of staying," Ambrose said again. But he thought of the small signs that he'd missed. Olivia had joined the book club that Kate ran at the library on Tuesday nights and she'd bought saddlebags for the bike — pink with yellow and white daisies. Maron said she'd signed up for a working bee at the school next month as well. Would she bother to do that if she was leaving?

"I'm a bloody fool," he groaned, resting his head on his arms for a second.

It was still drizzling on Monday as Ambrose pedalled Olivia's bicycle, bright saddlebags and all, down the hill to school. His coat flapped around his legs and by the time he parked in the bike racks outside the front gates, his trousers were damp. It would be good to bring his car over, as the weather was prone to rain even in summer.

From his classroom he could see the ferry docked at the pier, the seas still too rough to brave the crossing between Aggie and the mainland.

"Mōrena, everyone, let's carry on with our stories from Friday, and I'll have the kōwhai group up the front with me," he said, turning to the class.

Of course, by Wednesday the rain had stopped and the ferry was running again, but Ambrose couldn't leave Maron in the lurch. He'd taken to leaving his phone in his satchel during the day so he wouldn't check it for messages constantly, but in any case, it seemed like he was still blocked. He felt like half of him was missing.

Glenn had found some spare tōtara in his garage and had turned it into a display shelf for the senior class, and on Friday afternoon he came into the classroom to secure it to the back wall.

"Mr McCafferty, are you going to judge the rat hunt this year?" Fern asked.

"The what?" Ambrose squeaked.

Glenn let out a laugh, which he managed to disguise as a cough. "The school has a competition every year to see who can catch the most rats," he said. "It's part of the eradication programme and has been running since I was a kid. Did you know, children, I held the record for the most rats for four years running? Thirty-two was my personal best."

"I got the prize for biggest teeth last year," Fern said, "but Amber got the most. She had twenty-six."

"Biggest teeth?" Ambrose said, his voice still sounding a little higher than normal. "How do you judge that?"

Glenn was grinning broadly. "Well, you bend down and examine them, of course. All the rats are laid out on the playground, in order from biggest to smallest. I'll look forward to seeing who you award the silkiest fur to."

"You've got to be sh— kidding me," Ambrose muttered.

There was the deep bellow of a horn, and he looked out

the window to see the ferry getting ready to leave. A handful of people stood on the dock preparing to embark. Weeble unhooked the gate to let them through.

"... I could tell you a lot of facts about rats," Glenn was saying smugly.

"Right then," Ambrose said, picking up his satchel. "Class, Mr Moa is going to take over for the rest of the afternoon. Anything you want to know about rats, ask away. I'm sure, seeing he's such an expert, he'll be thrilled to judge the competition as well."

"Huh? What the—" Glenn stood gaping at Ambrose, his hammer still clenched in one hand. The horn blasted again and a grin slowly spread across Glenn's face. "Go get your girl," he said.

Ambrose was already out the door.

Chapter 41

Liv had thought things were bad after the break-up with Connor, but she hadn't been in love with him. Not really, and definitely not towards the end. Ambrose was always on her mind; as she poured drinks at the bar, while she worked on Sean's PR, whenever she saw a cat, or walked past a school. She missed him. She missed the island and the hotel, she missed all the people and Mr Tiddles. She missed waking up to the sound of the birds and the ocean and the clear, star-filled sky. But most of all she missed Ambrose. She wondered if he missed her, or if he was glad that she had left.

She'd get over him, she told herself. She was strong, she wasn't going to wither and die without him. It just felt like it.

Liv had cried for a solid week. Long, draining crying sessions that were totally self-indulgent, but she couldn't seem to stop. Then she'd tried to decide what to do. She still needed to see a lawyer about signing the hotel over to Ambrose, but she'd focused first on getting a job.

As she'd suspected, Renfield Reed had made it difficult for her to get any work, but Sean had referred a couple of friends who had hired her for some smaller PR jobs, so she was hopeful that eventually she could get her own business going. Meanwhile, she'd swallowed her pride and gone down to The Sawdust Saloon and asked if they were hiring. It was bar work, and she had to wear an awful uniform of Daisy Duke shorts and a checked shirt with a hideous pink cowgirl hat, but the pay was okay and it kept her busy. Liv had taken the bar job reluctantly, but her bias had been somewhat misguided. The other staff, and especially Jeremy the owner, were actually pretty great. She'd quickly become good friends with them all and it was only the occasional sleazy customer that made her cringe.

Hopefully, soon she could go for a whole day and not think of Ambrose or how much her heart ached.

Liv was pouring frozen daiquiris when Connor strode into the bar, his presence catching a few eyes, a group of lads by the pool table nudging each other excitedly. He looked the same as always, handsome in that arrogant way, his stubble artful, outfit designer and hair made carefully messy with expensive styling gel. He gave her a smile, all teeth and well practised.

"I heard you were working here," Connor said, cocking his head. "Had to see it for myself. Liv, babe, come on."

"Hello, Connor," Liv said, trying to keep her voice even. She pulled out a tray from under the bar counter. "What can I get you?"

He made a scoffing sound. "I'm not here for a watered-down drink. I came to see you, babe."

Liv ignored the 'babe' and filled the tray with the drinks she'd prepared before sliding it over towards the edge of the bar. "Cassidy? Table four, please," she called.

Connor eyed the bar top and carefully leant his elbows on the very edge. "Seriously, Liv, I've come here for you. Even though you broke my heart, I'm willing to give you another chance." He reached out a hand to rest it on top of Liv's where she was wiping down the counter. She pulled hers back.

"Did I though?" she asked.

"Did you what?"

"Did I break your heart?" Liv watched his face closely. She hadn't really considered that Connor might have been legitimately upset over being turned down. There had been numerous photos of him since that day with leggy models on his arm, but perhaps he really had been hurt by her rejection. Even if he hadn't tried to contact her until now. "I'm sorry if that's true," she added more softly.

His face hardened. "Of course it's true," he said. "You made me look like a fucking loser, standing there in front of everyone. People mocked me. And I've had a shit season. The coaches have been riding my arse all year."

There was no mention of him missing her specifically, Liv noted. Or of love.

"Well, I'm sorry about that," she said, looking over at the tables behind him to see if anyone needed serving. One group had finished eating and their plates needed clearing and a couple of tradies had come in and were looking around for a seat.

"So, what do you say? Dad's retiring, so I can probably get your old job back. I heard you had to move in with your mum. That can't be fun and I bet you miss the apartment. I remember how much you loved my bath."

Liv thought of the bath. It was impressive, like something from a movie, but it was nothing like the one Ambrose had fixed up for her on Aggie. It didn't even come close. Just the thought of that bath, and what she and Ambrose had done in it, brought a lump to her throat.

"Sorry, Connor, but I'm really not interested," she said. She started to wipe the counter, hoping he'd take the hint and leave.

"What? Why not?" He looked a little incredulous. "Come on, Liv, I need you back. This is my career on the line. You were my lucky charm. And we looked good together."

Looked good together. Not *were* good together. Still no mention of missing her, or being in love with her, or being miserable without her.

"Everything okay here, Liv?" Jeremy asked, coming up behind her.

"Yeah, sorry, this won't take long," Liv told him. She turned back to Connor. "I really need to get back to work," she said. "But it was nice to see you."

"Come on, Liv, give it up," he said. "You can't seriously expect me to believe you'd rather work here in this shithole than be with me? I get it, you didn't want a public proposal, but don't try and play games, any woman would be lucky to have me. So let's cut the shit, shall we?"

"Can you hear yourself, Connor?" Liv was still holding the cloth she had been using. She considered throwing it at him but shoved it under the counter, picked up an empty tray and lifted the hatch separating the bar from the front of house.

Connor looked at her blankly for a second. Now that she was standing in front of him, he eyed her up and down, his gaze lingering on her bare legs in the short Daisy Dukes. "Last chance, babe, I'm not going to stand around in this dump all night waiting while you pretend you're over me." Except she was, Liv realised.

"Did you ever love me, or was I just a prop you needed for your image?"

"Of course I loved you. I could have had a hundred girls way hotter than you, if it was just about my image."

Loved. Past tense. But she knew he hadn't loved her. If anything, he'd loved the idea of her.

She had no idea why he was here now, this stupid pretence

at trying to get her back, but she suspected it was something his manager had suggested to make him look better, or maybe it was to save face. The great Connor Reed couldn't possibly be humiliated by a mere female. They'd get back together and then he'd publicly dump her but in a way that wouldn't make him look bad. He always did like to have the upper hand.

"Then good luck. Go and take your pick," she said.

"You've just blown the best offer you'll ever get, Olivia."

Connor trailed behind Liv as she cleared empty plates from a table, smiling at the ladies seated there, but most of them were gawking openly at Connor.

"You're Connor Reed," one of them said. She tucked a strand of hair behind her ear and re-crossed her legs so that her short skirt rode up even further. Where Liv's legs were pale from a winter on Agnes Island, this girl had legs as sleek and tanned as a bottle of Bondi Sands.

"I am." Connor flashed his smile and gave the group a look over. He must have decided the brunette addressing him was his best bet, as he leant closer. "And who are you?"

She giggled and held out a manicured hand. "I'm Lexie."

Liv moved away to where the tradies had found a table by the window and took their order. Connor stayed where he was.

She kept one eye on Connor as she went back behind the bar and started putting dirty glasses into the dishwasher. He'd pulled up a chair and was chatting to the women, one hand resting on Lexie's thigh. He whispered something to her. They stood, Lexie teetering on very high heels, and Connor put his arm around her, his hand resting right above her bum. He didn't even glance in Liv's direction as they walked towards the door.

Jeremy came out from the office and stood beside her, watching as they left, a gleam in his eye. "Hopefully that's the last we see of that dickhead. He was in here last night looking for you as well."

"Now that he's found me, I don't think he'll be back," Liv said.

"You might have to put up with seeing a bit of him in the news over the next little while, sorry." A sly smile spread across his face. "I've been in the office checking the video footage from last night. The rugby union have been getting fed up with Reed's drunken antics recently. I think they might be very interested when I forward the footage of him snorting coke off the bathroom counter."

Liv looked at him and they both started laughing.

"And if not, I'm sure the gossip magazines will be."

After work, she pulled up to her mother's house and turned off the car, then sat trying to dredge up some energy to face going inside.

Deirdre was trying her best. She'd even started to see an online therapist. She had told Liv it was so that one day she might be able to come over to Agnes Island and see the hotel. Obviously, that wasn't going to happen now, but Liv was really proud of her for trying, and for the first time in a long time, they had talked about her brother Jason and how much Deirdre grieved for him and blamed herself for his death.

But her mother still had a long way to go in her mental health battle, so when Liv got to the door, she stripped off her uniform as usual and bundled it up for the laundry.

"Is that you, Livvy?" her mum called, and Liv grinned a little. Who else would it be?

"Hi, Mum," she called back, trying to sound cheerful. She took off her sneakers and sprayed them, then headed down the hallway, dumping her clothes in the laundry basket as there was already a wash going.

"You have a visitor," Deirdre said as Liv came into the lounge. Her mother was playing hostess, standing in front of the coffee table, pouring tea, a tray with a milk jug and a plate of biscuits set in front of her. And there, perched on the edge of the plastic-lined couch, was Ambrose. In his underwear.

Liv stood frozen in the doorway, staring at him. She was only dimly aware that her mother was fully dressed and that she and Ambrose were practically naked. She didn't even have on matching underwear.

"What are you doing here?" she asked.

"I'll leave you to it, shall I?" Deirdre put down the teapot and gave Ambrose a warm smile. "It's been lovely to meet you."

Ambrose half rose from the chair, his hands sort of covering his front. "You too, Deirdre, I appreciate you letting me in."

He gave Liv a long look as he sat back down and sighed. "I would have been here sooner, but I didn't know where you were, and then the ferries weren't going, and I really wish you'd have answered my calls."

"It seemed best to make a clean break," Liv said. She was surprised when her words came out sounding perfectly normal. In her head they were dancing around like fireflies. "Look, do you think we should put on some clothes? This feels a little weird."

Ambrose shrugged. "I don't actually have any spare," he said. "Your mum put mine in the wash and when I left Aggie I was in a bit of a rush. I didn't have time to pack anything."

"Wait here," Liv said, going to the hall cupboard and getting them each a robe. She handed one to Ambrose and then put one on herself. "There, better?"

"Well, less distracting, anyway," he said.

"Look, I'm sorry I haven't sorted the legal stuff yet," she said. "I've been meaning to, only ..." She swallowed the lump in her throat, looking down at her hands, determined not to cry.

"Oh Liv," Ambrose said softly.

She looked up at him in surprise. "That's the first time you've called me Liv," she croaked out.

"Is it?" He cleared his throat. "I guess I was always trying to keep you at a distance in my mind. As a way to protect myself. But Liv, I am an utter idiot. I cannot tell you enough how much I regret my stupidity in assuming you were leaving when I heard you had a job with Sean."

"It was going to be remote."

"Yes, so I discovered," Ambrose said drily. "Like I said — utter idiot." He chewed on his bottom lip. "The thing is, I'm not used to feeling like this about someone. And I panicked when I thought you were going. I told my mother we weren't serious but I was really covering up for feeling like a fool for falling for you." He was blushing slightly, Liv noted, and her heart was in her throat. "I thought I was wrong, thinking you felt something for me too."

"I shouldn't have run away, should I?" she said. "Sean tells me I have a habit of taking off when things get to be too intense, and he's right."

"I'm so sorry," Ambrose said. "I hurt you, and I never want to do that, ever. Please come home. Hartwell is only half what it should be without you. I don't want to do it by myself. But together it would be amazing." He swallowed. "I really am so sorry."

"I'm sorry too." Liv said. "I miss you. And Mr Tiddles the third."

They stared at each other, Ambrose's mouth curling up in a faint smile.

"Now what?" Liv asked.

"Would now be a good time to tell you I love you?" Ambrose asked.

Liv grinned. She didn't think she'd ever stop smiling. "Go on then," she said, "you first."

So he did.

About the authors

Nikki and Kirsty are sisters from New Zealand who wrote several books. It was quite fun so here's number seven. You can find out more about us, and our other books, at **www.nikkiperryandkirstyroby.com**